ripple effect

time thriller trilogy

ripple effect

paul mccusker

ZONDERVAN.com/
AUTHORTRACKER
follow your favorite authors

Ripple Effect
Copyright © 2008 by Paul McCusker

Previously published by Lion Publishing/Cook Communications as *Sudden Switch*

Requests for information should be addressed to:

Zondervan, *Grand Rapids, Michigan 49530*

Library of Congress Cataloging-in-Publication Data

McCusker, Paul, 1958-
    [Sudden switch]
  Ripple effect / by Paul McCusker.
     p. cm. -- (Time thriller trilogy ; bk. 1)
    Summary: Fifteen-year-old Elizabeth suddenly finds herself in a parallel world
where she is called Sarah and is diagnosed as having amnesia, while the real Sarah has
taken Elizabeth's place and is in a coma.
    ISBN 978-0-310-71436-1 (softcover)
    [1. Space and time--Fiction. 2. Identity--Fiction. 3. Christian life--Fiction.] I. Title.
PZ7.M47841635Sv 2008
[Fic]--dc22

2008022161

Published in association with the literary agency of Alive Communications, Inc., 7680 Goddard Street, Suite 200, Colorado Springs, CO 80920. www.alivecommunications.com

Interior design by Christine Orejuela-Winkelman

Printed in the United States of America

08 09 10 11 12 13 14 • 23 22 21 20 19 18 17 16 15 14 13 12 11 10 9 8 7 6 5 4 3 2 1

Dedicated with deepest love to the real Elizabeth Sarah,
and to Buddy Owens for coming up with the missing piece.

"I'm running away," Elizabeth announced defiantly. She chomped a french fry in half.

Jeff looked up at her. He'd been absentmindedly swirling his straw in his malted milkshake while she complained about her parents, which she had been doing for the past half hour. "You're what?"

"You weren't listening, were you?"

"I was too."

"Then what did I say?" Elizabeth tucked a loose strand of her long brown hair behind her ear so it wouldn't fall into the puddle of ketchup next to her fries.

"You were complaining about how your mom and dad drive you crazy because your dad embarrassed you last night while you and Melissa Morgan were doing your history homework. And your dad lectured you for twenty minutes about ... about ..." He was stumped.

"Christian symbolism in the King Arthur legends," Elizabeth said.

"Yeah, except that you and Melissa were supposed to be studying the ... um — "

"French Revolution."

"Right, and Melissa finally made up an excuse to go home, and you were embarrassed and mad at your dad — "

"*As usual*," she said and savaged another french fry.

Jeff gave a sigh of relief. Elizabeth's pop quizzes were a lot tougher than anything they gave him at school. But it was hard for him to listen when she griped about her parents. Not having any parents of his own, Jeff didn't connect when Elizabeth went on and on about hers.

"Then what did I say?" she asked.

He was mid-suck on his straw and nearly blew the contents back into the glass. "Huh?"

"What did I say after that?"

"You said … uh …" He coughed, then glanced around the Fawlt Line Diner, hoping for inspiration or a way to change the subject. His eye was dazzled by the endless chrome, beveled mirrors, worn red upholstery, and checkered floor tiles. And it boasted Alice Dempsey, the world's oldest living waitress, dressed in her paper cap and red-striped uniform with white apron.

She had seen Jeff look up and now hustled over to their booth. She arrived smelling like burnt hamburgers and chewed her gum loudly. "You kids want anything else?"

Rescued, Jeff thought. "No, thank you," he said.

She cracked an internal bubble on her gum and dropped the check on the edge of the table. "See you tomorrow," Alice said.

"No, you won't," Elizabeth said under her breath. "I won't be here."

As she walked off, Alice shot a curious look back at Elizabeth. She was old, but she wasn't deaf.

"Take it easy," Jeff said to Elizabeth.

"I'm going to run away," she said, heavy rebuke in her tone. "If you'd been listening — "

"Aw, c'mon, Bits — " Jeff began. He'd called her "Bits" for as long as either of them could remember, all the way back to first grade. "It's not that bad."

"You try living with my mom and dad, and tell me it's not that bad."

"I know your folks," Jeff said. "They're a little quirky, that's all."

"Quirky! They're just plain weird. They're clueless about life in the real world. Did you know that my dad went to church last Sunday with his shirt on inside out?"

"It happens."

"And wearing his *bedroom slippers*?"

Jeff smiled. *Yeah, that's Alan Forde, all right*, he thought.

"Don't you dare smile," Elizabeth threatened, pointing a french fry at him. "It's not funny. His slippers are grass stained. Do you know why?"

"Because he does his gardening in his bedroom slippers."

Elizabeth threw up her hands. "That's right! He doesn't care. He doesn't care how he looks, what people think of him, or *anything*! And my mom doesn't even have the decency to be embarrassed for him. She thinks he's adorable! They're weird."

"They're just … *themselves*. They're — "

Elizabeth threw herself against the back of the red vinyl bench and groaned. "You don't understand."

"Sure I do!" Jeff said. "Your parents are no worse than Malcolm." Malcolm Dubbs was Jeff's father's cousin, on the English side of the family, and had been Jeff's guardian since his parents had died five years ago in a plane crash. As the last adult of the Dubbs family line, he came from England to take over the family fortune and estate. "He's quirky."

"But that's different. Malcolm is nice and sensitive and has that wonderful English accent," Elizabeth said, nearly swooning. Jeff's cousin was a heartthrob among some of the girls.

"Don't get yourself all worked up," Jeff said.

"*My* parents just go on and on about things I don't care about," she continued. "And if I hear the life-can't-be-taken-too-seriously-because-it's-just-a-small-part-of-a-bigger-picture lecture one more time, I'll go out of my mind."

Again Jeff restrained his smile. He knew that lecture well. Except his cousin Malcolm summarized the same idea in the phrase "the eternal perspective." All it meant was that there was a lot more to life than what we can see or experience with our senses. This world is a temporary stop on a journey to a truer, more *real* reality, he'd say — an *eternal* reality. "Look, your parents see things differently from most people. That's all," Jeff said, determined not to turn this gripe session into an Olympic event.

"They're from another planet," Elizabeth said. "Sometimes I think this whole town is. Haven't you figured it out yet?"

"I like Fawlt Line," Jeff said softly, afraid Elizabeth's complaints might offend some of the other regulars at the diner.

"Everybody's so ... so *oblivious*! Nobody even seems to notice how strange this place is."

Jeff shrugged. "It's just a town, Bits. Every town has its quirks."

"Is that your word of the day?" Elizabeth snapped. "These aren't just *quirks*, Jeffrey."

Jeff rolled his eyes. When she resorted to calling him Jeffrey, there was no reasoning with her. He rubbed the side of his face and absentmindedly pushed his fingers through his wavy black hair.

"What about Helen?" Elizabeth challenged him.

"Which Helen? You mean the volunteer at the information booth in the mall? That Helen?"

"I mean Helen the volunteer at the information booth in the mall *who thinks she's psychic*. That's who I mean." Elizabeth leaned over the Formica tabletop. Jeff moved her plate of fries and ketchup to one side. "She won't let you speak until she guesses what you're going to ask. And she's never right!"

Jeff shrugged.

"Our only life insurance agent has been dead for six years."

"Yeah, but — "

"And there's Walter Keenan. He's a professional proofreader

for park bench ads! He wanders around, making people move out of the way so he can do his job." Her voice was a shrill whisper.

"Ben Hearn only pays him to do that because he feels sorry for him. You know old Walter hasn't been the same since that shaving accident."

"But I heard he just got a job doing the same thing at a tattoo parlor!"

"I'm sure tattooists want to make sure their spelling is correct."

Elizabeth groaned and shook her head. "It's like Mayberry trapped in the Twilight Zone. I thought you'd understand. I thought you knew how nuts this town is." Elizabeth locked her gaze onto Jeff's.

He gazed back at her and, suddenly, the image of her large brown eyes, the faint freckles on her upturned nose, her full lips, made him want to kiss her. He wasn't sure why — they'd been friends for so long that she'd probably laugh at him if he ever actually did it — but the urge was still there.

"It's not such a bad place," he managed to say.

"I've had enough of this town," she said. "Of my parents. Of all the weirdness. I'm fifteen years old and I wanna be a normal kid with normal problems. Are you coming with me or not?"

Jeff cocked an eyebrow. "To where?"

"To wherever I run away to," she replied. "I'm serious about this, Jeff. I'm getting all my money together and going some-where normal. We can take your Volkswagen and — "

"Listen, Bits," Jeff interrupted, "I know how you feel. But we can't just run away. Where would we go? What would we do?"

"And who are you all of a sudden: Mr. Responsibility? You *never* know where you're going or what you're doing. You're our very own Huck Finn."

"That's ridiculous."

"Not according to Mr. Vidler."

"Mr. Vidler said that?" Jeff asked defensively, wondering why their English teacher would be talking about him to Elizabeth.

"He says it's because you don't have parents, and Malcolm doesn't care what you do."

Jeff grunted. He didn't like the idea of Mr. Vidler discussing him like that. And Malcolm certainly cared a great deal about what he did.

Elizabeth continued. "So why should you care where we go or what we do? Let's just get out of here."

"But, Bits, it's stupid and — "

"No! I'm not listening to you," Elizabeth shouted and hit the tabletop with the palms of her hands. Silence washed over the diner like a wave as everyone turned to look.

"Keep it down, will you?" Jeff whispered fiercely.

"Either you go with me, or stay here and rot in this town. It's up to you."

Jeff looked away. It was unusual for them to argue. And when they did, it was usually Jeff who gave in. Like now. "I don't know," he said quietly.

Elizabeth also softened her tone. "If you're going, then meet me at the Old Saw Mill by the edge of the river tonight at ten." She paused, then added, "I'm going whether you come with me or not."

2

Jeff lived with his cousin Malcolm in a cottage where the north edge of town connected with the south edge of the vast Dubbs estate. The estate, owned by the Dubbs family since the eighteenth century, included a mansion, extensive lawns and gardens, hundreds of acres of forest, and a few rolling hills. The mansion was once the social center of the entire area. Now it was a museum — where no one lived, but lots of tourists came to visit.

Though he was the master of the Dubbs family fortune, Malcolm chose to live modestly in the cottage. Without a wife or children, he believed he didn't need to live in the "big house." Besides, he liked the coziness of the cottage and thought it suited him perfectly, even reminding him a bit of England. Jeff had joined him there right after Jeff's parents died.

Jeff entered the den where his cousin, tall and lean, was hunched like a weeping willow over a large desk. The sun had set, and a single banker's lamp illuminated the desktop with a greenish glow. The slight flicker from a neglected mound of hot coals in the fireplace cast stark shadows that danced around the cluttered room with its old-fashioned furniture, dark wood paneling, shelves spilling over with books, and paintings and drawings thrown randomly on the walls.

The clock on the mantelpiece struck the quarter hour. "Malcolm?" Jeff said.

"It's not right, Jeff," Malcolm said. "It's still not right. Come and see."

Jeff crossed the room, knowing full well what his cousin was talking about. On the desk were the plans for a "Time Village" — a theme park dedicated to history. It had become Malcolm's dream to use part of the Dubbs family's estate for an educational use. Malcolm's intention was to bring in homes, farms, and buildings from all over the world that represented different time periods, brick by brick. He would then fill those structures with anything and everything — from furniture to hair brushes — to make them authentic. Malcolm had all the money and resources he needed to pull the scheme off. Jeff knew he would succeed.

His cousin pointed to the left side of the drawing where someone had roughly sketched in a cluster of houses. "Do you think it makes sense to put the British mining village of the 1850s right next to the 1790 French farmhouse?"

Jeff looked closely at the plans and said, "It makes about as much sense as putting that New England schoolhouse from 1908 next to the blacksmith shop from 1672."

"Exactly! It makes no sense at all!" Malcolm exclaimed in his British accent. He smiled and his blue eyes were bright, reminding Jeff of his father. "People should come into the Village and move from point to point chronologically through time! That way they see the growth and development of culture and civilization."

Jeff nodded.

Malcolm folded his arms. "I'll tell the contractor that I don't care how much it costs to redo the landscape. If we're going to build this village, we must build it right."

"Right," Jeff agreed.

Malcolm turned away from the plans to face Jeff. "And what may I do for you?" he asked pleasantly. "I know you didn't come in here to talk about my village."

"I have a problem," Jeff said.

"Oh?" Malcolm tipped his head toward a chair. "Then you'd better sit down."

As Jeff slid into the cushioned embrace of one of the thick wingback chairs, he felt a familiar sense of relief. He knew he could talk to his cousin about anything. He also knew he would get a direct and honest answer. And though some folks in town thought Malcolm Dubbs was a little off-the-wall and unsuitable to raise a child, Jeff couldn't imagine a better substitute for the parents who could never be replaced.

"It's Elizabeth," Jeff said. "She wants to run away."

"Does she? To where?"

Jeff shrugged. "I don't know. She says her parents are driving her crazy and she wants to live somewhere normal."

"Normal?" Malcolm laughed. "And I assume she wants you to run away with her to find that mythical place?"

"How did you know?"

His cousin shrugged. "You've been friends a very long time. It makes sense that she'd want your help."

Jeff shook his head. "She's not asking for my help. She doesn't want anybody's help. She's so ... so ..." He groaned. "Independent."

"Do you think so?" Malcolm asked.

"Yes!" he replied and looked at Malcolm doubtfully. "Don't you?"

Malcolm smiled. "I believe Elizabeth likes people to *think* she's independent, but she's not. She needs other people just the same as you or I do." He paused, gazing at Jeff. "Well, are you going to do it?"

Jeff was startled. "What?"

"Are you going to run away with Elizabeth?"

"You're joking, right? I couldn't run away with her."

"Why not?"

Jeff was surprised by the question. "Well, I know she doesn't have much money. And I sure don't have any, except for my trust fund." He knew he couldn't touch that until he was twenty-one. "So I don't know where we'd go or what we'd do or how we'd survive."

"That makes sense," Malcolm said. "But what if you had the money? What if I said I'd give it to you?"

"Are you trying to talk me into leaving?" Jeff asked.

"I'm only wondering," said his cousin. "If money were no object, would you go?"

"No," Jeff said. "I mean, I understand her feelings, and why she wants to run away, but I think she's really running from one problem to a whole bunch of new ones."

Malcolm gazed at his nephew for a moment. "You're a smart lad. Did you say all of this to her?"

"Well, no."

"Then you should."

Jeff shook his head. "She won't listen to me."

"You're her closest friend. If she won't listen to you, she won't listen to anybody," Malcolm said. "When is she planning to go?"

"She said to meet her at the Old Saw Mill at ten o'clock."

"Then meet her — and make her see the good sense of *your* plan to run away."

"Do I have a plan?" Jeff asked, puzzled.

"You certainly do. Running away makes perfect sense once she's saved her money, attained her education, determined where she's going and what she'll do when she gets there ..."

"But that's not running away," Jeff said. "That's growing up and moving out."

"Exactly!" Malcolm declared. "And perhaps by the time she does all that, she'll realize how much her parents love her — even if they do drive her mad."

Jeff looked at his cousin with deep admiration. "You know, Malcolm, I want to be just like you — when you grow up."

"Then you'll have a long wait," he said. "I don't intend to grow up."

Jeff rose to his feet. "Thanks."

"Don't thank me. You're the one who came up with the answers."

Jeff walked to the door.

Malcolm cleared his throat. "Now, don't forget that I'm leaving tomorrow for Washington, D.C. I'm not sure how long I'll be gone. You have my cell phone. Or if it's a real emergency, Mrs. Packer will be around."

Mrs. Packer was their housekeeper.

"Okay."

As if it were an afterthought, Malcolm added, "Oh, and if Elizabeth won't listen to reason — simply tie her up, drag her home, and lock her in her room until she comes to her senses."

"Yes, sir." Jeff grinned. As he reached for the knob, he suddenly turned back. "Malcolm, do you think I'm anything at all like Huck Finn?"

"Huck Finn? Not at all. You're far more intelligent than Huck Finn. Why do you ask?"

"No reason," Jeff said and closed the door behind him.

3

Elizabeth didn't want to take a bath.

But it seemed to be the only refuge for her frayed nerves. She was angry with Jeff for not agreeing to run away with her. And once she returned home, her folks seemed unusually attentive to her, as if they knew she was up to something. *It's that old "parents' radar" again*, she thought. *Somehow they know when they're not wanted and insist on staying close by.*

Her father, who normally besieged her with lectures about a new discovery in the garden or a particular Greek phrase he had translated from an old manuscript, had apparently decided that tonight (of all nights) he would ask her questions about her day at school.

Then her mother said she'd heard that Elizabeth and Jeff had some sort of quarrel at the diner. How had that news reached home even before she did? Small towns were unbelievable ... and Fawlt Line was surely among the worst. Her mother said she was concerned because Elizabeth and Jeff never quarreled. Was everything all right? Elizabeth mumbled a vague response and excused herself to go to her room.

She had just begun to look in her closet for good running-away clothes when her mother came in. More questions. "Are you feeling all right? Are you sure you don't want to talk about what happened with Jeff? You seem unhappy about something, Elizabeth. What is it?"

Elizabeth ran out of evasive answers and announced that she was going to take a bath. It was her only escape; the only reprieve for her tense muscles and tangled emotions.

As she stepped into the bathroom that adjoined her bedroom, Elizabeth turned to glance at her mother. The woman stood in the center of the bedroom, a worried expression on her face, her hands knotted in front of her. The muted yellow light of the bedside lamp cast shadows that intensified the wrinkles on her face. She looked old.

Her mother sighed. "Your father and I have a meeting at church. We'll be back in an hour or so."

"Okay, Mom." Elizabeth closed the door and turned the key in the lock.

Her robe, its limp arms dangling in a gesture of resignation, hung carelessly from a hook on the white wooden door. Elizabeth spun the chrome clover-shaped faucet handles. The spigot spat, the pipes groaned, and the water roared into the milky-white claw-footed tub. She wiggled her fingers under the waterfall to test the temperature, then pinned her dark hair up into a bun. She considered peeking to see if her mother was still outside the door, but dismissed the thought. It would only trigger more questions.

Cautiously she touched a toe to the water. Not too hot, not too cold — just right, like the littlest bear's porridge. She stepped into the tub and sat down, stretching her long legs as far as they could go. The tub was too short and made bald islands of her knees. She put her head back, and the steam rose around her. The water licked at her chin. Her skin was prickly velvet. She closed her eyes and let her thoughts run.

Would Jeff meet her at the Old Saw Mill? No. He wouldn't run away. Why would he? His life with Malcolm was ideal, no weird parents to embarrass him. He didn't know what it was like for her.

She looked across the still bath water. Though she hadn't moved, the water suddenly rippled as if someone had tapped the side of the tub with a tack hammer. It settled again. She pushed a stray lock of hair away from her eyes and slid deeper into the water.

He probably went home and talked to his cousin, she thought. Malcolm would give him all the reasons Elizabeth shouldn't run away. It wasn't smart. They had no money. How would they survive?

Well, how did anyone ever survive? she argued with him in her mind. They'd figure it out as they went along. And making money should be easy enough. There were plenty of odd jobs for kids their age to do.

But —

She knew what Malcolm would say; he was always the voice of reason. *Be honest with yourself.* She squeezed her eyes closed, hoping to block his voice out. *You don't know the first thing about surviving. You don't know how to make any money. Your parents have always given you an allowance. Where will you go? What will you do? What's so terrible about your life?*

You don't know, she answered. *You don't understand.*

I know, I understand.

Her internal argument made her feel tense again. She lifted up her right foot just as a drop of water fell from the tap. It splashed cold against her skin. She sighed and closed her eyes.

Was the voice right? Was her life really so bad? Would running away only make things worse for her? The first cracks of doubt appeared on the surface of her determination. Did she really know what she was getting herself into?

Suddenly rough hands grabbed her, hard fingers wrapped around her throat, pressing tight, pushing her under icy water.

Elizabeth gasped and opened her eyes, startled and alarmed. She glanced around. The bathroom was unchanged.

Where in the world did that thought come from? she wondered, now breathing rapidly.

She tried to reconstruct the image in her mind, but it was a blur. Rough hands around her throat. No air. No breath.

How bizarre, she thought as she tried to calm down. She didn't usually have violent thoughts or imaginings, regardless of how tense she felt. *I'm just upset*, she concluded. She glanced down into the bath and instantly recoiled, jerking her legs up with a shriek.

The water was filthy brown with bits of grass and sludge floating on top as if a sewer had backed up through the drain. Her stomach turned and she grabbed the sides of the tub to pull herself out. She pushed up, but couldn't get her footing on the slick porcelain. Her legs splayed out and she lost her grip. Her body crashed downward, sliding toward the front of the tub. Her head dipped under the water and hit against the curved bottom. She thrashed out, her hands clawing at something, anything. Getting a hold on the edge of the tub, she pulled herself up with all her strength, and catapulted over the side onto the cold tiled floor. The water spilled with her, splashing all around. She lay on her side, coughing and sputtering. She wanted to scream for her dad, but couldn't find the breath to do it.

What happened? How could —? Her mind was tangled with the impossibility of what had happened.

She got her breathing under control and sat up. Her hip protested by sending a sharp pain down her leg. She examined it closely. *That'll be a doozy of a bruise by morning*. She peered into the tub for a look at the water. It was gone. The tub was bone dry.

A dream. I must've fallen asleep in the bath and slipped under the water. Of course. I let the water out. I've been lying here for a long time. It's the only thing that makes sense.

On unsteady legs she stood up and pulled the towel from the rack to dry herself. She then dropped the towel on the floor and pushed it around with her foot to mop up the puddles she'd made. She felt herself calming down. The whole thing seemed absurd. She wanted to laugh out loud. *What will Jeff say when I tell him about this?* He'd probably scold her for falling asleep in the bath.

Still, the violent image of rough hands strangling her flashed in and out of her mind. Rough hands, the strangling feeling, brown water.

She turned to the small shelf above the toilet tank where she had placed a pair of clean panties and a T-shirt. They weren't there. *That's funny,* she thought. *I'm sure I brought some in.* She glanced around. She must've left them in the bedroom. She reached for the robe hanging on the door. It was gone too.

Wait a minute, she said to herself. *I may have forgotten my T-shirt and panties, but I know the robe was there.* Suddenly, she was unsure of herself. *Am I dreaming?*

She opened the door. The bathroom light spilled into the dark bedroom. She moved slowly, sure she'd left a light on. Maybe her mother had turned it off before she left.

Elizabeth made her way to her dresser and opened the top drawer. She retrieved some panties and a t-shirt. In the closet, she found a robe, but it was unfamiliar to her. Probably one of her mother's resale shop finds. She put it on and it fit.

She sat down on the edge of the bed, trying to pinpoint why she still felt so odd. A leftover feeling from what had happened in the tub, perhaps. But something was wrong. Her room *felt* different to her.

She heard footsteps in the hall and her skin went goose-pimply. Her parents were supposed to be at church.

There was a shadow of feet under the closed door.

"Mom?" she whispered, surprised at how her voice caught in her throat.

The door slowly opened. Even by the dim light from the

bathroom, she could make out the shape and shadowy details of the face.

It wasn't her mom. Or her dad.

Elizabeth put a hand to her mouth to stifle her scream even as the stranger glanced toward the bathroom, and then suddenly snapped his head in her direction. His eyes grew wide.

They both screamed.

4

The stranger stumbled backward and fumbled for the light switch.

Elizabeth threw herself across the bed and grabbed a lamp from the bedstead, not for light but to use as a weapon.

The overhead light came on, dazzling her eyes with its brightness. She squinted. Her assailant hadn't moved from the door.

"What do you want?" she shouted.

"Want?" he asked softly. He seemed genuinely confused.

She blinked, her eyes getting used to the light. The stranger was clearer now: young, maybe sixteen years old, stocky, and wearing a white Oxford shirt and dark trousers. His face had a set, square look, his eyes were wide with bewilderment, and his short blonde hair stuck out in several directions as if a comb of static had passed through it. He stretched out his arm in a silent appeal and his mouth moved, but no words came out.

To Elizabeth's surprise, he looked truly shocked.

"I'll call the police!" She reached toward the bedstead for her phone. It wasn't there.

Something is wrong, something is different.

Elizabeth's senses were fully alive in these fast-moving seconds, relaying more signals than her mind could take in. *Something is wrong, something is different.* The room was arranged the same, the placement of the bed and the dressers were where they belonged. But the coloring was all wrong. The curtains were a busier, darker pattern than hers. The dressers were a lighter oak instead of the rich, red cherry that she loved.

"If you know what's good for you, you'll get out of here now. My parents will be walking through the front door any second now!" She tried to sound tough, but her voice quivered.

"Your parents?" the stranger asked. "Sarah, what's the matter with you?"

"Nothing's wrong with *me*, bud. But you'll have plenty to tell the police!" She raised the lamp high and moved to the foot of the bed. If she could only get to the phone in her parents' room. *At least, I hope there's still a phone in my parents' room.*

"Sarah, listen to me — "

"Back away from the door," she said. "Go toward the bathroom."

The young man's arms were still outstretched, his palms turned upward in entreaty. He obeyed her. He stepped from the door and moved backward toward the bathroom.

As Elizabeth rounded the foot of the bed, the lamp's electrical cord reached its limit. The lamp jerked from her hand and crashed to the floor. With a loud pop the bulb shattered and the light went out.

Elizabeth screamed and ran through the doorway into the hallway. Again, in an instant, she was aware of how different it seemed — like her home, and at the same time unlike it. She banged into a small unfamiliar table with an equally unfamiliar potted plant on top. The plant tipped over and a collection of framed photos scattered to the floor. She stumbled and fell on her backside next to them.

The strange young man peeked around the doorway. Spying her on the floor, he took a cautious step into the hall. "Sarah, listen to me," he said calmly. "I don't understand what's going on. Why are you here? Are you playing some kind of game?"

"Stay away from me!" Elizabeth said, crawling away from him.

From the bottom of the stairs a woman called out, "Calvin? Calvin, is everything all right?"

Startled, Elizabeth opened her mouth to shout for help. But before she could, the young man responded.

"Yeah, Mom! I'm just talking to Sarah," he called back.

"Is she back? I didn't hear her come in," the woman replied.

He turned to Elizabeth again. "Sarah, please. Don't upset my parents again."

"Why are you calling me that?" Elizabeth snapped.

"What do you want me to call you?" he asked. He cocked his head slightly. "Are you hurt? Why are you acting so strange?"

"I'm fine!" she snapped. What was going on here? This young man — this Calvin — stood in the doorway as if ... as if he *belonged* there. He didn't look threatened or worried. He looked perfectly at home.

"Let's talk about it," he offered and took another step toward her, his hand out to help her up.

"Stay back!" Elizabeth cried, panicking. Why couldn't she sort out what was happening? Did she really believe that in the short time she was in the bath, this stranger had somehow redecorated her home and brought in some woman to pretend to be his mother? It didn't make sense. Nothing made sense. "I'm going to call the police," she said.

The young man frowned. "All right. But you'll only embarrass yourself. Do you want me to take you to the phone?" He moved toward her.

She growled at him, "Keep away from me. I don't know who you are or what you want, but *stay away!*" Her eyes darted about to see if there was anything within reach that might serve as a means to protect herself. Her gaze fell onto one of the tumbled photo frames. In it was a photograph that made her mouth go dry and filled her with a sense of wild panic.

The photo was of the stranger sitting on a blanket in a large grassy field. A picnic was spread out nearby. He was holding up a glass as if making a toast. And sitting next to him, smiling happily was ...

"Me! This is me," she gasped, leaning back against the banister.

There was no denying it — there were the two of them in the same photo, sharing some happy memory on a bright summer's day somewhere.

She swayed unsteadily, the photo moving in and out of focus. She lowered her head. "What's going on here?" she mumbled. Had she come out of the tub in some sort of sleepwalking trance and wandered into someone else's house? Had she hit her head on the tub and, even now, was dreaming ... or in a coma ... or drowning?

She put a hand to her head and turned toward the stranger. "Where am I? Who are you?"

"I don't understand," he said, watching her anxiously. "You really don't know, do you?"

"I wouldn't ask if I knew!"

He raised his hands again. "Okay, I'll play along. My name is Calvin Collins."

"Calvin Collins," she repeated. The name meant nothing to her.

"Calvin Collins?" he persisted. "You know. I'm your boyfriend."

Elizabeth slumped to the floor.

5

"I'm losing my mind," Elizabeth whispered.

Calvin stooped next to her. He reached out to touch her shoulder, then apparently thought better of it and withdrew his hand. "What happened? Why are you acting like this?" he asked gently.

"I want my parents," she said. "I want Jeff." Her whole body shook. She looked Calvin full in the face, but couldn't manage to say anything else.

"Maybe I should take you to the hospital," Calvin said. "I don't know what's going on, Sarah, but — "

"Don't call me that!" she cried out with a choked-off whimper. She drew her knees up to her chest, wrapped her arms around them, and began to rock.

"But that's your name. Sarah Bishop. Who do you think you are?"

She shook her head. "Where am I?"

Calvin moved from his crouching position and sat down next to her on the worn carpet. "You're in my house — well, it's my parents' house. You moved in after your mom and dad ..." He looked away uncomfortably. "After they were killed in a car accident. Don't you remember?"

How can I remember something that didn't happen? Or did it? Were her parents killed, and now she was deep in some kind of psychotic shock or denial? "I don't remember. It doesn't make sense. I took a bath, that's all. I took a bath, and when I came out, everything was different." Her voice sounded shrill to her ears, the way she imagined a voice would sound when a person was on the edge of a nervous breakdown.

"Maybe you *did* fall in the tub and hit your head," Calvin suggested. "I've read about stuff like that.. Maybe you have some kind of amnesia. Come on, I'll take you to the hospital. You might be hurt in ways we can't see."

Elizabeth nodded; maybe a doctor could figure this out. She rose unsteadily to her feet. "Okay. But I'd like to use your phone first. Maybe if I try to call my parents — "

"But your parents are dead," Calvin insisted.

"Let me try!" Elizabeth screamed.

He guided her down the hall and into a room. It should have been her parents' bedroom. It even had the same out-of-style wallpaper with dull yellow flowers on a rose background. She fought back the tears as she picked up the receiver and dialed her home number. Hope rose somewhere deep within her as she heard the phone ring once ... twice ... three times ... and then it was picked up on the other end.

"Hello?" said a thin, masculine voice.

It wasn't her father.

"May I speak with Alan or Jane Forde, please?"

"You have the wrong number." *Click* — he hung up.

"Come on, Sarah," Calvin said.

Elizabeth clenched her teeth and dialed the number again, wanting to be certain. The same masculine voice answered and, when she asked for the Fordes, hung up, annoyed at being bothered a second time. She slammed down the phone, then picked it up and frantically dialed Jeff's number — Melissa's number — Karen's number — every number she could think of. But she didn't know anyone and, worse, wasn't known by anyone.

Finally Calvin took the phone from her hand and put his arm around her to guide her out of the room.

The tears burned as they spilled from her eyes, and there was a howling in her ears that she recognized as her own voice crying out, crying out into a darkness that sucked her swirling and spinning into it until her body fell forward, into a darkness without relief.

6

Alan Forde wasn't easily alarmed. But as he stood knocking on his daughter's bathroom door, it was definitely alarm that he felt. Elizabeth had started her bath before he and his wife left for church over an hour and a half ago. There was no sign that she'd ever come out.

He knocked again. "Elizabeth!"

There was no answer apart from the soft echo of a drop of water hitting a tub full of water. He turned the handle and pushed on the door. It was locked.

"What should we do?" his wife asked from behind him. "Should I call someone?"

"No," he said as he turned the handle again and threw his weight against the door. He had never thought of Elizabeth as the suicidal type. But she had been acting so strange all evening and maybe ... maybe ...

"Alan!" Jane sobbed, her small fist against her lips.

Alan was an ox of a man, over six feet tall, 225 pounds of solid flesh and bone. He wasn't about to be defeated by a wooden door. He backed up and threw his shoulder against it again. And again. And again, until he heard the snap of the catch and the wrenching of the supporting screws. Once, then twice more and it cracked and splintered, the door flying open. Alan, off-balance, nearly crashed to the bathroom floor. He grabbed the towel rack to steady himself.

"Elizabeth!"

Her T-shirt and panties were neatly folded near the toilet tank. The shower curtain was drawn around the tub. *She fell asleep in the tub!* Alan thought. *Dear God, don't let her drown.* He threw the shower curtain aside with such force that it popped away from several rings.

The tub was full of water — the spigot continued to drip indifferently — but Elizabeth wasn't there.

Jane put her hand to her mouth.

Alan reached down to feel the water. It was cold. He stood up straight and put his hands on his hips. A locked door, an empty, windowless bathroom, cold water . . . *where was Elizabeth?*

His analytical mind flipped through the possibilities like so many index cards in a box. Jane raced from the bathroom. Alan could hear her screaming Elizabeth's name throughout the house.

Alan shook his head. *She's not here.* He knew without knowing how he knew. *She's gone.*

On feet that seemed somehow disconnected from the rest of his body, Alan walked to the phone on Elizabeth's bedside table. He wanted to believe that there was a simple explanation for all this. He sat down on the edge of her bed and searched through the debris of her untidiness. Past a half-read novel, a stained mug, and scattered note paper, he found her address book.

"Elizabeth!" his wife shouted frantically from the other end of the house.

Alan picked up the receiver and systematically called everyone in his daughter's address book. First the names he recognized, and then the names he didn't. One by one they gave the same answer: no, they hadn't seen her.

A solitary tear slid from his eye, journeyed down the bridge of his nose, and fell onto his grass-stained bedroom slipper.

7

Elizabeth sat numbly in the passenger seat of Calvin's compact car, watching the familiar lights of an unfamiliar city spin past. Calvin was talking, but she caught only snippets of what he said.

"Your name is Sarah . . . you're my girlfriend . . ."

"I want to go home," she said.

"We're almost at the hospital," Calvin said. He was quiet for a moment. "Don't you remember *anything*?"

I took a bath, she wanted to explain. *That was all. I thought somebody grabbed me, tried to drown me. The water was dirty. I slipped and hit my head on the bottom of the tub. And when I came out, everything was different.* But she said nothing.

"Tell me more about who you think you are, Sarah," Calvin said.

"Elizabeth," she said sharply, hoping that the sound of her own voice saying her own name would bring her back to reality. "My name is Elizabeth Forde. My mom and dad are Jane and Alan Forde . . ." It was all she could say. Panic and tears stole her voice.

"It's all right," Calvin said calmly. "We'll get a doctor to look at you."

"I took a bath," she whispered, barely audible above the hum of the car motor. "Maybe I hit my head under the water."

Calvin looked at her as if startled by the revelation. "Maybe you did," he agreed. "A doctor will know."

———

But the doctor on duty at the emergency room *didn't* know, Elizabeth realized quickly. He made humming noises and probed, muttering that her scalp showed no sign of cuts, bruises, or swelling. "A slight bump on the back, but incidental," he observed to no one as his cold hands moved around her skull. He checked the bones in her face. "You think you fell asleep in the tub? Maybe bumped your head, huh?"

"Maybe," Elizabeth answered. She knotted her hands in her lap, her fingers touching and twisting the leg of the cotton sweatpants she had on — Sarah's, just like the pullover sweater Calvin offered her. And the white socks and the sneakers. All a perfect fit.

The doctor — *Dr. Stewart*, his badge said — grunted, then went through the routine of checking her pupils. "Size ... equality ... reactivity ..." he murmured. "No discoloration ..." Her ears and nose were next, then her mouth. "No blood ... no unusual fluids ..."

With a nurse assisting, the doctor checked Elizabeth's neck and chest, abdomen, lower back, and her lower and upper extremities. He noted the bruise on the side of her leg and scribbled as she explained how she had slipped and fallen in the bathroom. Apart from the bruise, she felt no pain at all, only the awkward discomfort of having her body examined by a complete stranger.

"Tell me again what happened," Dr. Stewart insisted.

Elizabeth chewed at her lower lip. She explained that she took a bath after her parents left for a meeting at church. She was planning to see Jeff a little later.

Dr. Stewart gestured to Calvin. "This is Jeff?"

"No," Elizabeth said.

"I'm *Calvin*," Calvin said, chagrined. "Her *boyfriend*."

Dr. Stewart mumbled to himself and scratched his chin with the top of his pen. "Then what?"

"In the bath I — " Elizabeth stopped, unsure of how much to say about what she had imagined in the tub. *They'll think I'm crazy.* "I think I slipped and hit my head. I'm not sure."

Dr. Stewart waved his pen at Calvin. "You were in the house when she took her bath? You didn't hear anything?"

"I didn't know she was in the tub," Calvin replied. "I thought she was out and — "

"She went out?" the doctor asked.

"I went out?" Elizabeth asked, surprised.

"Earlier, yeah," Calvin admitted.

"With Jeff?" the doctor asked.

"I don't know anybody named Jeff," Calvin said, a touch annoyed. "She said she was going to a movie by herself. She does it all the time. Maybe she took a bath when she got home. I don't know. I don't know anything except that I peeked into her room later and . . . and she was like this."

Elizabeth shook her head. "I hate to go to movies by myself. I had a bad day with my parents and took a bath to relax."

"So you've said," Dr. Stewart said.

"But her parents are dead," Calvin said quickly.

"Are they?" the doctor said, his eyebrows lifting up dramatically. He looked at Elizabeth. "How long have your parents been dead?"

"They're *not* dead," she said.

Dr. Stewart's eyebrows fell into a frown. "They're either dead or they're not, young lady. Your boyfriend seems to think they are."

"He's *not* my boyfriend," Elizabeth said.

Groaning, Dr. Stewart shoved his pen into his pocket. "Let's see what some X-rays will tell us."

8

At the Old Saw Mill, Jeff woke up with a start. He had fallen asleep in a corner where he had a clear view of the door. He didn't want to miss Elizabeth when she came in. He twitched his nose at the cobwebs and coughed at the overwhelming smell of rotten wood. Outside, he could hear the river splashing over the rocks.

He looked at his watch. Twenty-five past ten. Where was Elizabeth? Did she give up on her idea to run away? Then why hadn't she given him a call on his cell phone and spared him the trip?

He heard something outside and suddenly realized that a noise had awakened him. The sound of car tires on gravel. And now a car door slammed shut.

He scrambled to his feet just as two uniformed police officers burst through the door, scouted the area, and raced toward him. He backed against the wall.

"Don't move," one of the officers commanded and roughly grabbed his arm.

Jeff yelped, but didn't struggle. "What's going on?" he asked.

A third man stepped through the door and frowned at the officer. "You don't have to manhandle him, Bill."

The officer let go of Jeff's arm.

"You two check the area," the third man ordered. The officers obeyed, and the man in charge turned his attention to Jeff. "Hi, Jeff," he said. Jeff recognized him from photos in the newspaper. He was Richard Hounslow, Fawlt Line's new sheriff. He was a mountain of a man with a round, boyish face, wavy brown hair, and the kind of pleasant, no-nonsense attitude you'd expect from a small-town law officer. *Andy Griffith on steroids.*

"What's wrong? Was I trespassing? I didn't see any signs," Jeff said.

"What're you doing out here?"

Jeff swallowed hard. "Well, I came out to ... take a walk and then I got tired and thought I'd come in here and ... and ..." He didn't believe a word of it himself.

"You haven't seen Elizabeth Forde, have you?" Sheriff Hounslow asked.

"Elizabeth? No," he answered honestly. "Why?"

"She's missing, and we thought you might know something about it."

"Missing!" His mind raced. Had she decided to run away on her own?

Sheriff Hounslow hooked his thumbs in his pockets. "Look, Jeff, there's no point in acting innocent. Alice Dempsey at the diner overheard you two talking about meeting out here tonight." He stopped and chuckled. "Though she thought you said you were going to Old *Sawyer's.*"

Jeff rolled his eyes. Sawyer's was the name of the drugstore on Main Street. Leave it to Alice to mishear what she'd overheard.

"We figured it out," the sheriff said, growing serious again. "Where's Elizabeth?"

Jeff shrugged. "I don't know. I mean, it's true we were going to meet here. She was mad at her parents and wanted to run away. But I was planning to talk her out of it."

"So where is she?"

"I don't know. Did you check her house?"

"Her dad called us. That's what started this whole thing. Her folks are understandably very upset. Now why don't you come clean and tell me where she is?"

Jeff was worried. If she wasn't at home and hadn't come to meet him, then something *was* wrong. "I don't know," he insisted.

And he continued to insist he didn't know all the way to the police station.

9

"The X-rays are clean as a whistle," Dr. Stewart announced. "There's nothing there that would lead me to conclude that you've suffered any shock or injury. Now, I'm no neurologist — "

"Then who is?" Calvin asked. "Let's talk to him."

"We're a small hospital. We can't afford round-the-clock neurologists. You can try Uniontown, or you can come back tomorrow when Dr. Kennedy is here."

"Tomorrow?" said Elizabeth. Was it possible that she might still be in this strange situation tomorrow? *No. I'll be awake by tomorrow, and this nightmare will be over.*

Dr. Stewart rubbed his eyes wearily and spoke to Calvin. "I have a problem here. This girl has no identification, but has admitted that she's underage. You're not a relative and for me to do any more than I've done, I need a guardian's approval. But I honestly don't think there's anything left for me to do in lieu of any physical signs of trouble."

"What are you saying?" Elizabeth asked.

"Get a good night's sleep and come back tomorrow," Dr. Stewart replied as he scribbled on his pad. "You'll want to talk to Dr. Waite."

"Who's Dr. Waite?" Calvin asked. "You said the neurologist is Dr. Kennedy."

"Dr. Waite is not a neurologist. He's a psychiatrist," said Dr. Stewart.

"I'm not crazy," Elizabeth insisted through clenched teeth.

Dr. Stewart smiled patiently. "I didn't say you are. But there's clearly a problem beyond any physical cause, so the psychiatric wing is our next step for a look over."

"A look over for *what*?" Elizabeth demanded.

"For something other than a physical cause. An emotional trauma. Amnesia. I don't know." Dr. Stewart turned to Calvin, his smile frozen in place. "See that she meets with Dr. Waite."

Calvin nodded silently.

Elizabeth pounded the diagnostic table. "He's not my keeper!"

"Look, I've done all I can," Dr. Stewart said, his voice showing the first crack in his patience. "I'd love to try to figure this out for you but, frankly, I have emergencies waiting." He turned on his heel and marched out of the room.

Elizabeth didn't move.

"Sarah — " Calvin began, then stopped. "I don't know what's happening here. This makes as much sense to me as it does to you. But we should do what he said. Let's go home, and in the morning — "

"What home?" Elizabeth snapped. "I don't have a home."

"Okay, fine. If you're not comfortable at my house, I can take you to a friend's — "

"What friends? Do I have any friends?"

"A hotel, if that's what you want. Though I don't know what we'll find at this time of night." He watched her silently, then spread his hands in appeal. "Now, this is just a suggestion — don't be offended. I think you should come back to my house for the night. *You* don't remember, but Sarah considered it home. I promise that we'll take care of you. And in the morning we'll come see this quack Dr. Waite."

Elizabeth looked up at him and noticed for the first time that his eyes were blue. Like Jeff's. She wanted to trust him. Under the circumstances, what other choice did she have?

"All right," she said. "Thank you."

Calvin sighed deeply, relieved. "I'm just so happy that you came back to me."

⎯⎯⎯

The sun was rising as Elizabeth and Calvin drove back to Calvin's house. In the dim light of dawn, Elizabeth had a better chance to look at the town. It was both familiar and unfamiliar, like a picture that someone had tampered with — correct in most respects, but altered just enough to seem false. Buildings were in the wrong places, names changed, even one-way streets reversed. The gas station where she and Jeff once stopped to put air in their bicycle tires was now a fast food restaurant. The abandoned bowling alley that was due for demolition was a pristine multi-screen movie theater complex. How was it possible?

"This *is* Fawlt Line, isn't it?" Elizabeth asked after they passed what should have been the Fawlt Line Diner but was now called "Hank's."

"You remember Fawlt Line? Hey, we're making progress!" Calvin said.

"Fawlt Line is the name of *my* town too," Elizabeth replied.

Calvin frowned.

They pulled up the driveway to Calvin's house and, as they approached the front porch, Elizabeth felt the same disjointed sense of reality. The house was Victorian just like her's, but parts of it were shifted around. The chimney that should have thrust up from the living room on the left side was now sticking out of some other room on the right. Windows were in odd places. The color was a different shade of gray. Even the stained-glass window above the front door had changed from an elaborate rose to a coat of arms.

Calvin's parents, Ted and Barbara Collins, were waiting for

them at the kitchen table, dressed in bathrobes and looking like unmade beds.

"Well?" Mrs. Collins asked as she sipped her coffee without looking at either of them.

"We'll get some sleep and then take her back to see another doctor," Calvin answered.

"I don't like this," Mr. Collins said in a scratchy morning voice. He turned to Calvin, speaking as if Elizabeth wasn't there. "So help me, if this is another one of her stunts ..."

Her stunts? "I don't know what you're talking about," Elizabeth said.

Mr. Collins glared at her.

"We'll talk later," Calvin snapped, and took Elizabeth's arm, pulling her out of the kitchen.

"I'm so sorry," Elizabeth said. "I wish I knew what was happening here. I wish I — " Their looks of surprise stopped her from finishing.

"She's learned how to apologize," Mrs. Collins said with a snort.

"Now there's a miracle," Mr. Collins replied.

Calvin tugged Elizabeth to the stairs. "Don't listen to them," he said.

"What did I do to offend them?"

"Nothing. Forget about it," he said.

She followed Calvin up to her room — or Sarah's, she thought. It felt like a lifetime since she had come out of the tub and into this strange dream.

Calvin gestured around the room like a bellboy to a new guest in a hotel. "The bathroom is there and your bed's there. Maybe you'll remember more after you've had some sleep."

"Maybe I will," Elizabeth said, but she didn't believe it.

Calvin took a step forward, reaching for her hand. Elizabeth stepped back, nearly tripping over the lamp she had broken earlier.

"The mess . . ."

"I'll clean it up later," he said.

"I'll do it," Elizabeth offered.

"Will you?" He looked puzzled. "You'll clean it up."

"Of course," she replied. "I broke the lamp — the least I can do is clean it up. Why are you looking at me like that?"

"It's not the kind of thing you've ever offered to do."

What kind of girl is this Sarah? Elizabeth wondered, then shrugged. "I'm offering now."

"Okay." Calvin moved to the doorway. "I'll wake you in a few hours."

"Thank you," Elizabeth said gently, and meant it. What would she have done if he hadn't been so nice to her?

He smiled sadly and pulled the door closed.

The familiarity of the bathroom gave her the creeps. She was tempted to take another bath in the hope that it would somehow send her back to her own home — like Dorothy tapping her red shoes in *The Wizard of Oz.*

She leaned over the sink and looked at her puffy, tired face in the mirror. Had she lost her mind? Did she really need to talk to a psychiatrist?

The doctor had suggested she might have amnesia.

Was that possible? As far as Elizabeth knew, amnesiacs were people who had *lost* their memories completely. She'd never heard of an amnesiac who lost one set of memories for another set. If she really were Sarah, then where in the world did all of Elizabeth's memories come from? She had a lifetime of them. And all too clearly she remembered that last fight with her mom and dad, and her conversation with Jeff at the diner. She was going to run away from home.

It looks like I succeeded, she thought.

The weight of it all overcame her and, suddenly exhausted, she made her way to bed. She was surprised to find Calvin there, laying out fresh clothes for her. He spun around apologetically.

"Sorry — I thought maybe you wouldn't remember where your clothes were."

"I probably wouldn't have."

"I know it's a stupid thing to think about, but — " Calvin blushed. "It occurred to me that you don't have your purse. Do you know where it is?"

"My purse? No, I don't know where it is." Elizabeth was perplexed. If she couldn't remember her own name, why would he expect her to remember where her purse was?

"Like I said, it's a stupid thing to think about." He backed toward the door. "It really is good to have you home again."

Again?

10

Sheriff Hounslow led Jeff into a stark, windowless interrogation room in the Fawlt Line police station, a gray granite fortress in the center of town. The building and the room itself had all the charm of a medieval torture chamber.

"You want anything to drink?" Hounslow asked.

Jeff said thanks, but no, and the sheriff walked out. Jeff paced for a moment, then sat down in one of the metal folding chairs next to the scarred wooden table. The fluorescent light flickered above him. That — plus the industrial green walls — made him feel seasick. Or maybe he was nervous. He'd never been questioned by the police before.

What weighed on his mind even more, though, was Elizabeth. He wracked his brain for possible explanations, but nothing fit. She *must* have run away on her own. What other explanation was there?

No. Jeff didn't believe it. She wouldn't run away without letting someone know, without someone's help. Sure, she could be stubborn and independent, but not so much that she'd run away alone. Something was definitely wrong.

The door opened and Alan and Jane Forde were escorted in by Sheriff Hounslow. "Please sit down," the sheriff said, gesturing to the remaining chairs.

Mr. Forde glanced around the room, then at Jeff. He managed

a faint smile. Jeff smiled back. Mrs. Forde looked at him silently through puffy eyes. Hers was the face of every dark thought and every worry any of them could have about Elizabeth. It made Jeff's heart take a downward turn.

Mr. Forde pulled out a chair for his wife to sit on. She grabbed the table as if the effort would send her to the floor instead. Struck by an unaccountable feeling of responsibility, Jeff looked away at one of the windowless walls and wished his cousin were there. But Malcolm was well on his way to Washington, Jeff knew. He wondered if the police had called Mrs. Packer.

"Coffee for anyone?" Sheriff Hounslow asked politely.

They all shook their heads no.

The sheriff waited until all eyes were on him. "I'm sorry, Alan — Jane. I know how difficult this is for you," he said. "Maybe Jeff will be so kind as to tell us everything he knows about Elizabeth. Maybe he'll start by telling us where she is right now."

Surprised at the sheriff's insinuation, Jeff looked up at him, then across the table at Mr. and Mrs. Forde. "I don't know where she is," Jeff said. "Honest. If I did, I'd tell you."

Hounslow propped his leg on the remaining chair. "I'd like to believe you, Jeff. But I know how close you two were and … well, you'd do anything for Elizabeth, wouldn't you?"

"Almost anything."

"Like keep a secret? Y'know, if she asked you not to tell anyone where she was, then you might not tell, right?"

Jeff shook his head. "This is too serious. I'd tell you."

Hounslow leaned forward, resting his elbow on his knee. "Okay, then, Jeff. Go ahead and explain to Mr. and Mrs. Forde what you were doing at the Old Saw Mill."

"I was waiting for Elizabeth to meet me," Jeff admitted.

In an identical movement, Mr. and Mrs. Forde turned to face Jeff. "Why?" Mr. Forde asked.

"She had a plan to run away from home — the two of us, I

mean," Jeff said, looking down at the tabletop. "But I wasn't going to do it. I was going to talk her out of it."

"Why did she want to run away from home?" Mrs. Forde whispered.

Jeff shrugged. "You know how Elizabeth is. She got mad and decided to leave."

"Who was she mad at?" Mr. Forde asked.

Jeff didn't want to answer the question. He didn't want to get into family squabbles at a time like this. He looked helplessly at the sheriff, hoping he'd intervene, but Hounslow merely cocked an eyebrow in response.

"At you two," Jeff finally said.

Mrs. Forde opened her mouth to react, but Mr. Forde put his hand on her arm and nodded, as if no further explanation were needed. "What do we do now, Sheriff?"

Hounslow sat up straight. "If we're willing to believe that Jeff doesn't know where she is — "

"Jeff wouldn't lie," Mr. Forde said simply. "So let's get on with whatever we have to do."

The sheriff scratched his cheek. "Then maybe you should tell me why Elizabeth was mad at you."

Mr. Forde stared at Hounslow for a moment. It was hard to tell if Hounslow was asking a routine question or implying more. Mr. Forde cleared his throat. "Unless Jeff can say otherwise, I believe that I'm an endless source of embarrassment to my daughter."

All eyes fell to Jeff, as if he might disagree. Instead he blushed.

Mr. Forde went on. "I can't believe she would run away, though. I can't be so unbearable that she'd — " He fell silent and slumped in his chair a little.

"Shouldn't we be out looking for her?" Mrs. Forde asked in a strained voice that betrayed her frayed emotions.

Sheriff Hounslow looked indifferent. "Maybe she's gone off on her own for a while. It happens with teenage girls."

"No," Mrs. Forde snapped. "*No one* has heard from her — something is *wrong!*"

Hounslow stood up. "We can do some checking around, but technically I can't issue a missing person's report for at least twenty-four hours. I suggest you go home so you'll be there when she cools down and comes back."

Mr. Forde sat up straight and looked as if he might argue. Then, apparently changing his mind, he stood. After helping Mrs. Forde out of her chair, he said to Jeff, "If you hear from her, you'll let us know?"

"Yes, sir," Jeff replied.

Mr. and Mrs. Forde slowly walked out of the room. "God help us," Mrs. Forde whispered as they disappeared around the corner.

"Are you sure there isn't anything else you want to tell me?" the sheriff asked Jeff suspiciously.

"No," Jeff said.

"You had some kind of fight at the diner, didn't you?"

Jeff bristled. "We didn't have a *fight*. Elizabeth and I don't fight. She was mad at her parents, I told you."

Sheriff Hounslow gestured for Jeff to stand. "I'll have one of the boys take you home. Maybe your cousin has some suggestions. He seems to know everything there is to know about everything." The hint of sarcasm was hard to miss.

"Malcolm's out of town," Jeff said coldly.

"Too bad," the sheriff said. "I'm sure he could impress us all and find Elizabeth in no time."

That's more than you're willing to do, Jeff thought. *And since you won't look for her, I will.*

———

Mrs. Packer was waiting for Jeff when he walked through the front door. Her disheveled hair and untidy robe told him that she'd been roused suddenly from her bed. Her stern face looked even sterner when framed by the tight strands of white hair that had sprung loose from their pins. Her lips were pressed tight.

Jeff wondered, not for the first time, why Malcolm liked her so much. She gave Jeff the creeps.

"Malcolm called from his hotel room in Washington," she said as if the call's being long-distance made it all the more inconvenient to her. "He wanted to know how your evening went with Elizabeth. I told him that she's missing."

"How did you know?"

"The police came here to see if you knew where she was," Mrs. Packer said.

"Oh, I'm sorry," Jeff said.

"So you should be," she said. "Things like this wouldn't happen if you kids weren't allowed to run loose at all hours of the evening — "

"Did Malcolm leave a message?" Jeff asked.

She frowned at losing her chance to lecture him. "He said he's sorry and that he'll speak with you tomorrow."

"Is that all?" He had hoped Malcolm would jump on the first plane home. Sarcastic or not, Sheriff Hounslow was right. Malcolm *could* find Elizabeth. "Is that all he said?"

"Is that all?" Mrs. Packer cried out indignantly as she gathered up the bottom of her robe and marched up the stairs. "Nothing is ever good enough for you!"

She was right, Jeff thought. He slipped out the front door and into the cool night to find Elizabeth.

11

If there had been any doubt before, there wasn't now. Dr. Kenneth Waite, a dark-haired man with piercing blue eyes and a "staff psychiatrist" badge on his white coat, was certain. "You have amnesia," he said.

"Amnesia," she repeated.

"But it's not the kind of amnesia you've seen on television — where the hero gets conked on the head and forgets who he is until someone conks him on the head again," Dr. Waite explained. "It's hysterical amnesia."

"I'm not hysterical," Elizabeth said with a great calm.

The doctor leaned back in his chair and threaded his fingers together. "It's a stress-induced amnesia brought on by a mental trauma."

"What kind of trauma?" Calvin asked from the guest chair next to Elizabeth.

Dr. Waite nodded as if he appreciated the intelligence of Calvin's question. "We've seen it in cases of abuse or rape, where the victim goes into deep denial not only about the event itself, but his or her entire life. Other cases have included the sudden death of a loved one — "

"Your parents!" Calvin blurted to Elizabeth. "Maybe it's a delayed reaction."

Elizabeth cringed.

"Maybe," Dr. Waite allowed. "Trauma comes in many forms."

After hours of sitting on cold hospital carts, enduring endless questions, getting her head scanned by bizarre-looking machines, and struggling to keep her sanity in this nightmare, she had had enough. "You want trauma? I'll give you one: how about a girl takes a bath and when she gets out of the tub finds herself in a completely different world where everyone calls her by someone else's name? That's a trauma for you."

Dr. Waite smiled indulgently from across his large oak desk. "Sarah — "

"Elizabeth," she corrected him.

"The sooner you accept this situation, the sooner we can begin the healing process."

"If you want to heal me, then figure out how to get me home!" Elizabeth shouted, rising to her feet.

Calvin shifted in his seat nervously. "What about that? I mean, you say she's got amnesia, but she remembers all kinds of things. But they're things that she never did."

"I did too!" Elizabeth said, arms folded.

Dr. Waite leaned forward. "In certain types of trauma, resulting in this type of amnesia, it's not uncommon for the patient to create an alternative memory — or, shall we say, *reality* — that seems happier or more preferable to the reality that he or she is in. We call that *paramnesia*, where dreams or fantasies become the reality."

"You're making this up as you go along, aren't you?" Elizabeth said.

"So what do we do?" Calvin asked.

"I think we should admit her to the hospital for observation," Dr. Waite said. "Perhaps try a session with sodium amobarbital."

"Uh-uh." Elizabeth shook her head. "You're not going to drug me up and put me in the loony ward," she said.

"It's not a loony ward," Dr. Waite explained. "It merely has other patients who also have non-aggressive psychological conditions."

"No. I won't do it."

Dr. Waite tapped the leather blotter on his desk. "Legally, we don't need your permission, Sarah. As your legal guardians, Calvin's parents have already signed the forms. But I'd rather have you agree."

Elizabeth's face was set.

"I thought you wanted to go home," Dr. Waite said.

"I do."

"Then this may be the way to get there."

"What're you talking about?"

"*If* you are Elizabeth and this is, as you say, some kind of nightmare, then we may be able to wake you out of it. For all you know, I am really a doctor from *your* reality trying to reach you through your consciousness. The same is true if you are Sarah, somehow lost in a dream called Elizabeth. Either way, we want to bring the *real* person back to where she belongs. And time spent here will help us to do that."

Elizabeth eyed him skeptically. It made sense in a strange, psychobabble sort of way. "But you're not going to spend all your time trying to convince me that I'm Sarah, right?"

Dr. Waite shook his head slowly. "We won't try to convince you of anything. We'll let Elizabeth and Sarah take care of that."

———

"I get a room of my own?" Elizabeth asked as Dr. Waite got her settled in a plain white cell off the psychiatric wing. Calvin had gone home to get her clothes, toothbrush, and toiletries. "I thought these loony bin rooms were always shared."

"Your boyfriend says his family will spare no expense for you," Dr. Waite replied.

Elizabeth remembered the cold, uncaring expressions on Calvin's parents' faces and couldn't imagine that they would give her a dime, let alone an expensive room in a hospital.

"I must warn you," Dr. Waite said from the doorway, "that

people will call you Sarah. It's the only name they know. Your — er, *her* friends will come to visit. You need to be understanding if they don't acknowledge you as Elizabeth."

Elizabeth shrugged. "I'll cope."

"Good. Let me know if you need anything." He strolled into the hall, looking first in both directions as if checking traffic at a pedestrian crossing.

Elizabeth sat on the edge of the pristine bed and looked around at the cold, sterile room with its assembled metal and Formica furniture on wheels. *There's no place like home,* she thought, mentally tapping red shoes.

She had promised herself when she woke up that morning to play it tough. No crying, complaining, or whining. She'd be a rock, no matter what happened. That was the way to be. Tough as nails.

In her heart she held the tiny hope that she might be able to will herself out of this dream.

And it was a dream. She knew that now. Dr. Waite himself had used the phrase. It was a dream and, if she were strong enough and could look it in the eyes long enough, she would wake herself up. She must simply be strong and hold on to what she knew to be true. *I am Elizabeth. Elizabeth. Elizabeth.*

"Sarah?"

Elizabeth looked up and suddenly realized that she was not sitting on the edge of the bed, but lying on her side, her arms folded, her legs pulled up to her chest.

A pretty girl with deep dimples and short brown hair stood in the doorway. She was wearing a loose striped pullover sweater, jeans, and white tennis shoes. She smiled, but her large eyes betrayed uneasiness. "Hi ya," she said.

Elizabeth slid off the bed and stood next to it, not wanting to venture too far from its safety. "Are you a nurse?"

The pretty girl looked crestfallen for a moment, but recovered quickly. "No. Don't you remember me?"

"Sorry," Elizabeth said. "I don't remember anything that people think I should remember."

"Huh?"

Elizabeth waved to a chair. "I guess you can sit down if you know me. Maybe you can tell me something about myself."

The pretty girl moved to the chair but stopped midway. She was closer to Elizabeth now and spoke in a low whisper. "You really don't remember me? I mean, this isn't one of your stunts, is it?"

One of your stunts. One of her stunts. So it wasn't just Calvin's parents who suspected Sarah's behavior.

"I don't know what you're talking about," Elizabeth said.

The pretty girl resumed her walk to the chair and sat down. "It's okay. I was just checking. I heard what happened and, well, I didn't know what to believe."

"Look, I don't mean to be rude," Elizabeth said, "but who are you?"

"Rhonda."

Elizabeth wished the name would trigger her memory. But the wish immediately scared her and she retracted it. How could she wish for a memory as Sarah that she knew couldn't be real as Elizabeth? This Rhonda Whoever-she-is was a stranger. *Elizabeth* didn't know her.

"I'm sorry. How do I know you?"

The pretty girl called Rhonda chuckled. "Seriously?"

"Seriously."

Rhonda smiled, her dimples deeply angelic. "I'm your best friend."

The phrase *best friend* caught Elizabeth off guard, unexpectedly bringing to mind the best friends that she had had in her life. Karen Adams. Michelle Warburg. Melissa Morgan.

But one best friend in particular filled her thoughts. Jeff. Jeff, who was supposed to meet her at the Old Saw Mill. Jeff, whom she could count on and confide in and complain to, whom she considered her best friend above and beyond the call of best friend duty. Jeff. Would she ever see him again?

With the image of his face, the rock of her resolve shattered, the supposedly tough nails bent and broke. Elizabeth found herself weeping in the arms of this other best friend whom she had only just met.

12

The *Fawlt Line Daily Gazette* ran the story about Elizabeth's disappearance. It even mentioned that she had "disappeared" from a locked bathroom while in a tub full of water. The entire town talked about it in the shops and restaurants. The consensus was that Elizabeth had taken off for a new life somewhere, probably in the "big city." (What "big city" they were talking about was never made clear.) Even Helen, the supposedly psychic information booth volunteer, was quoted as saying she had a feeling that Elizabeth was long gone.

Jeff resented the gossip and speculation. Elizabeth was gone, but he was certain she hadn't run away. She was in trouble. Maybe kidnapped. Maybe ...

Jeff shuddered to think about it.

Searchers combed the woods, empty buildings, shacks, old wells — anywhere she might have accidentally gotten herself trapped — or hidden on purpose. Every neighborhood, block, lone street or alleyway, country lane, and abandoned tract of land was explored. Jeff investigated on his own, checking places that he and Elizabeth had been, even places they'd only talked about. Anywhere Jeff could think of, he searched.

At eleven o'clock that morning, the town reacted to a rumor that Elizabeth was seen in the company of an older dark-haired man with a tattoo on his forearm at the Park & Dine Truck Stop way out on Route 40. The police found the man and his companion at the truck stop, all right — only "Elizabeth" was a sixty-three-year-old woman in a black wig.

Mr. and Mrs. Forde offered a reward to anyone who could provide information. Jeff ached for them. He could imagine how terrible they felt, losing their daughter and suspecting that it was somehow their fault. He wished he could say something to comfort them, but he wasn't very good at talking to adults. With the exception of Malcolm, they made him uneasy. Especially Sheriff Hounslow.

The sheriff had stopped by first thing that morning to ask Jeff more questions. Jeff was sick of repeating his story. What was Sheriff Hounslow doing, trying to trick him into some kind of confession?

As the day went on, Jeff had to wonder: was it his imagination, or was he seeing the sheriff at unexpected times in unexpected places? Police cars showed up as he rounded a street corner in his Volkswagen, or stepped out of a shop. Jeff wasn't paranoid enough to believe they were following him. But maybe they were. Maybe they thought he knew where Elizabeth was, and hoped to catch him meeting her.

The issue was put to rest late in the afternoon when Jeff arrived at home. As he put the key into the door lock, someone tapped his shoulder. It was the sheriff.

"Hi, Jeff," he said. "Okay if we talk for a couple of minutes?"

"I guess so," Jeff said, but he didn't invite the sheriff into the house. They remained on the porch.

"I'd like you to tell me again about your last conversation with Elizabeth and why you were waiting for her at the Old Saw Mill."

Jeff sighed impatiently. "How many times do I have to tell you?"

"As many times as it takes, I guess," the sheriff said pleasantly.

"Why? Do you suspect me of something? Do you think you'll catch me in a lie? *What do you really want to know?*"

Sheriff Hounslow hitched his thumbs in his belt and leaned against the doorpost. "Put yourself in my position, Jeff. Besides her parents, you're the last person who talked to Elizabeth. And according to witnesses, you had an argument — "

"We *didn't* have an argument!"

"A heated discussion then — I don't care what you call it. All I know is that the customers there saw what they saw. Then her parents report her as missing. We also learn that she was supposed to meet you at the Old Saw Mill. And, lo and behold, we find you waiting for her there. But there's no sign of Elizabeth — anywhere. What are my options?"

Jeff didn't answer. He knew the sheriff would tell him anyway.

"My options are that Elizabeth really did run away by herself. But you and her parents say she wouldn't do that. What am I supposed to think? She was kidnapped? There's no ransom note, no phone call. And nobody saw any strangers around town that day or evening, so I'm not inclined to think that she's in the clutches of some maniac.

"So it comes back to you. You're her best friend, and you were going to help her run away. So I'm thinking that maybe she's hiding somewhere, and you know where but you're not saying."

"That's not true — "

"Yeah, yeah, save your protest." Sheriff Hounslow stood up straight again. "But if I were a big-city detective, I might not be so trusting. I might think that you're not telling us the whole truth about your argument at the diner or why you were meeting Elizabeth at the Old Saw Mill. I might even think that something worse happened between you."

So it was out, Jeff thought. This was what the sheriff was after. He felt the heat rise through his entire body, flushing his cheeks and breaking a sweat on his brow. "You think I did something to her?"

"I'm just saying what I *might* think under certain circumstances, that's all."

Jeff's eyes burned. All day he had felt trapped between the hope that Elizabeth would suddenly turn up and the fear that she was gone for good. All day he had searched with a knot in the pit of his stomach that he might find her — but not safe or healthy. All day he had hoped for the best but expected the worst. That's what he had learned to do after his parents died; it was the only way to cope with life. But he *never* expected to be a suspect in Elizabeth's disappearance. He clenched his teeth as the anger rushed to his tongue. He tried to hold it back.

"Something you want to say to me, Jeff?" Sheriff Hounslow asked.

Jeff opened his mouth to rail against his accuser. Suddenly the front door opened. Jeff and the sheriff both turned, surprised by the interruption.

Malcolm smiled at his nephew. "Hello, Jeff."

"You're home!"

"So I am," he acknowledged, then turned a hard look toward the sheriff. "If you're going to persist in questioning my ward, then we'll all go down to your office and I'll make sure a lawyer is present."

Hounslow coughed nervously and said, "It's not necessary, Malcolm. We were just having a friendly chat."

"Uh huh," Malcolm said. "Well, if you'll excuse us, Jeff and I also need to have a friendly chat."

Hounslow nodded to Malcolm, shot a fiery glance at Jeff, and strode off the porch and down the walk.

Relieved, Jeff blew out his cheeks and wiped his forehead. "Malcolm — "

"I know." Malcolm smiled. "He takes his job very seriously."

"He thinks *I* did something to Elizabeth!"

Malcolm put his hand on Jeff's shoulder. "Don't let it bother you. He has to be suspicious — that's part of his job too. But, if it's not too much trouble, I want you to come in and tell me everything that happened after I left."

13

"I had a dream last night that all the buttons came off my dress. I rushed for my sewing kit, and when I found it, I realized that all my fingers were gone. I had two bumpy stumps instead of hands with fingers. And I was upset because I couldn't sew the buttons back on my dress. I woke up screaming." The silver-haired woman dropped her head onto her chest as if reliving the dream had drained her of all her energy.

Elizabeth shifted nervously in an uncomfortable wooden chair, one of a half dozen chairs gathered in a semicircle for Dr. Waite's afternoon therapy group.

Another woman in her early thirties detailed her adventures as a silent movie screen actress in a previous life. She also announced that, in a life before that, she was Genghis Khan.

A man with jet-black, greased-back hair and chiseled face told the group how he'd seen his dead wife on the bus yesterday afternoon. Apparently he'd forgotten that he hadn't been out of the hospital for weeks.

An old man with kind eyes and thin lines of white hair pasted across a spotted scalp remembered the day a bomb killed his family during the London Blitz. Dr. Waite smiled indulgently and reminded the man that he has never been out of the country, let alone in London during a war. "Oh," the man said, accepting the correction passively. "My mistake."

All Elizabeth could think, now that she had heard four different stories like this, was that she was definitely in the wrong place. She didn't belong here with this group of mixed nuts. What did her particular nightmare have to do with the neurotic dreams and strange compulsions of these poor mentally disturbed people? She was not mentally disturbed.

Or was she? Suddenly Elizabeth realized that, to Dr. Waite, Calvin, and everyone else, her denial of being Sarah — her insistence that she had another life as someone called Elizabeth — must sound exactly like these testimonies sounded to her. *Insane*.

She brooded on that thought as a hospital maintenance worker in white overalls entered. He glanced apologetically at Dr. Waite and the group, but Elizabeth was the only one who took any notice. Her first impression was that he was an older man, his thinning dark hair sprayed with white throughout. But as she got a better look at his face, she noticed that his face seemed much younger. Then it struck her: *He looks like a young man trapped in an old man's body.* The worker moved quickly to a table at the far end of the room and busied himself stacking a tray of dirty coffee cups.

Dr. Waite cleared his throat, and Elizabeth was aware that all eyes were on her. "We're waiting to hear from you," he said softly.

"What do you want me to say?"

"Why not start with your name?" he answered. It was a challenge.

She sat up straight in her uncomfortable wooden chair. "My name is Elizabeth, but everyone seems to think I'm someone else named Sarah." She faltered for a moment until Dr. Waite encouraged her to tell the group everything she could. Reluctantly, she did — beginning with her life with her dad and mom in Fawlt Line, continuing with the bath, and ending at the point where Calvin brought her to the hospital. The group nodded at her with great understanding. The Genghis Khan-turned-silent-movie-star dabbed a tissue at her eyes.

Elizabeth felt like crying too. The last thing she wanted was the affirmation of these whackos.

Dr. Waite announced to the group that their purpose was to help synthesize Elizabeth and Sarah into one whole and healthy person. He never used the term "hysterical amnesia," but it hung over his carefully chosen words.

At least he kept his promise, Elizabeth thought. *He isn't trying to convert me into believing I'm Sarah.* But she felt discouraged and unsure of herself. Cups rattled as the hospital maintenance man disappeared out the door with his tray.

Okay, let's be honest for a minute, she thought. What if she stepped outside of herself and looked realistically at her situation, just for a minute? There she is, a young girl whom everyone knows as Sarah. There's Calvin and his parents, her "best friend" Rhonda, and no doubt scores of others who have individual memories of her as Sarah. They could each tell stories about her, present an entire history of her life that's completely flawless in its truthfulness. To the entire world, she is Sarah. But she alone insists that she's Elizabeth. She alone has memories of her mother and father, Jeff, her Fawlt Line ...

The therapy group ended, and the worm of doubt followed Elizabeth back to her room. She was startled to find several bouquets of flowers, all accompanied by expressions of love from Calvin. And he had brought in framed photographs — of her alone, of her with him. The happy couple.

She was touched but not comforted. Which *she* was she looking at? Was it Elizabeth in those photos or Sarah?

Elizabeth stared at a picture of herself — of Sarah — with Calvin. In it her hair was a different style, shorter. She looked younger. Calvin looked younger too, and less beefy. But they looked very happy.

"That was taken right after you moved in with my family," Calvin said from over her shoulder.

Elizabeth glanced up at him, then locked her eyes on the photo again. "I'm sorry. I don't remember."

"That's okay," he said. "You will. And even if you don't, I believe we can start all over again. Maybe it's even better this way. A second chance to do everything right. To fix the things that went wrong." He put his hands on her shoulders. "I love you, whoever you are. I want you to know that."

Elizabeth moved away from him, to get his hands off of her shoulders. She went to the window, which looked out onto a parking lot filled with cars that sparkled like jewels in the afternoon sun.

"It's too much to take in," Calvin said. "I know. Forget I said anything. How about business? Can we talk about business?"

"Business?"

"Nobody knows where your purse is."

Elizabeth was confused. "My purse?"

"It's gone. Maybe you took it out with you and left it somewhere. Who knows? We can't find it. But we need to make arrangements to get you some new identification. Y'know, driver's permit, credit card, and all that."

The importance and significance were lost to her. "Sure. Go ahead."

He scratched his chin. "So ... I should just have them replaced."

Elizabeth turned to face him again. "Yes," she said, puzzled.

"The identification will be in your name ... I mean, Sarah's name. You'll be Sarah."

Now she understood. The question of the day.

Are you Elizabeth or Sarah? Just who exactly are you?

The evidence of many witnesses ... the proof ... her own reason all told her that she must be Sarah. Whatever happened in the tub — whatever she thought she remembered as Elizabeth — was completely outweighed by the facts.

Elizabeth looked at Calvin. He had been so nice to her — kind, caring, even charming. She clenched and unclenched her fists. She thought about being held by Rhonda as she cried earlier. She thought of the reality of this room and the smell of the flowers and the view from the window. It was real. All of her senses said that it was. *So what are those other memories? What are those scenes and people and feelings from some other place?* The evidence was stacked up, layer upon layer, on her will and resolve. Even her own senses testified against her.

How could she withstand it and *not* go crazy?

Are you Elizabeth or Sarah?

Why not play along? See what happens?

Are you Elizabeth or Sarah?

At least there would be peace in a decision. She wouldn't be at war with a truth that seemed obvious to everyone but her.

Are you Elizabeth or Sarah?

"You win," she said to Calvin. "I'm Sarah."

14

In his cousin's study Jeff repeated exactly what had happened, beginning with his trip to the Old Saw Mill to wait for Elizabeth. Malcolm listened quietly. When Jeff finished his tale, he sank back into the solace of the thick-cushioned chair.

Mrs. Packer entered with a tray bearing a pot of hot tea. Jeff declined it, but Malcolm, with a thoughtful expression, poured milk into the extremely large mug that served as his "tea cup." Jeff relaxed. Somehow the very ordinary activity of having tea in his cousin's study gave him a sense of security, a refuge from the distress of the past day.

"You didn't mention one little item that the newspaper reported," Malcolm said to Jeff.

"What's that?"

"The locked bathroom door," Malcolm answered, sipping his tea. "That's the thing that gets my attention. I know the Fordes' house — at least its age. I assume the rooms still have doors that lock with keys."

Jeff had to think about it for a moment, then he nodded. "Yeah, they do."

"If Alan Forde is telling the truth, and I'm inclined to believe he is, then how could the door be locked from the inside without Elizabeth being in there?"

Jeff sat up. "I hadn't thought of that."

Malcolm rested his chin on his hand. With his bookshelves behind him, he looked as though he were posing for a portrait. "Why would Elizabeth go to all the trouble of filling the tub and somehow locking the door from the inside in order to run away? Also, according to the newspaper, Alan Forde said that none of her clothes were missing. What do you make of that?"

Jeff shook his head. "I don't know. What do *you* make of it?"

"If her plan was to run away, then she would have taken some of her belongings — certainly some of her clothes."

"That makes sense," Jeff said. "So she didn't run away. She was grabbed by someone."

"Taken from a locked bathroom? That's quite a trick."

"Then what happened to her? Where is she?"

"I have a theory," Malcolm said. "Though I don't expect anyone to believe it."

"Try me," Jeff offered.

Malcolm got out of his chair and paced with his head lifted up and his hands clasped behind his back. "Brace yourself, Jeff. You're going to need every ounce of imagination you can muster."

"Okay," Jeff said, not sure what he was getting himself into.

"For years I've been fascinated with various forms of paranormal and psychic phenomena. Not fortunetellers and freaks," he qualified with a raised finger, "but unexplainable experiences. History is filled with them. More than that, our little town has a history of them."

"What's that have to do with Elizabeth?"

Malcolm smiled. "I've been exploring the possibility of a relationship between certain states of mind and the very sudden unexplainable disappearances of people."

"You're kidding," Jeff said. "Are you going to tell me you think Elizabeth was kidnapped by aliens or something?"

"No."

"Good."

"But I could give you quite a lesson about missing persons. Not only individuals, but entire villages." Malcolm paced silently for a moment. "I've never told anyone about this, but I've put together a lot of pieces and discovered that Fawlt Line has its own strange history. There's a reason this town is so unusual, and I have a theory about that too. But for now I'll stick to disappearances. Like Charles Richards. Ever heard of him?"

Jeff hadn't.

"Charles was the grandson of Langham Richards, a big investor in tobacco in the nineteenth century. The family made a lot of money then, and well into the twentieth century. To everyone's chagrin, Charles Richards opted for a modest life as a farmer rather than becoming a wealthy merchant. That was interrupted by the Vietnam War. He was twenty-two years old and was drafted. In 1967 Charles came back from the service, built a house for himself, his wife, and two kids on a small farm just outside of Fawlt Line, and settled down to a life as a young gentleman farmer."

Jeff shifted in his chair. "I still don't understand what this has to do with Elizabeth."

"Bear with me," he continued. "One morning the two children, Susan and Donald, were playing next to the sidewalk — the one leading from the house to the front gate. Charles and his wife, Julia, stepped out of the front door. Charles had some errands to take care of at the bank in Fawlt Line. Charles kissed his wife good-bye and walked down the steps toward the kids. Julia stayed at the door, watching him. Charles patted his kids on their heads as he walked past. They giggled and waved. He reached the front gate, pausing as a car came up the road toward the house. It was driven by Dr. Hezekiah Beckett, the local veterinarian, who was dropping by to check on one of Charles' horses that had been sick. With him was a young boy who was helping the doctor that summer.

"Anyway, Charles waved at the doctor and paused to check

the time on his wristwatch. He then turned as if he were going to walk toward the approaching car to greet Dr. Beckett. He took three steps and, in full view of his wife, his children, Dr. Beckett, and the boy, *he disappeared.*"

"What do you mean by 'disappeared'?"

"I mean *vanished*, completely out of sight," Malcolm said. "His wife screamed. The children stood frozen. Dr. Beckett stopped the car, leapt out, and raced to the spot. A moment later Julia, the children, and the boy joined him. The five of them looked at the ground. They saw only the grass. No bushes, no trees to hide behind, no holes to fall into — nothing to give them any hint as to what had happened to Charles."

Jeff's wide eyes didn't move or blink. "You're kidding."

Malcolm went on. "Dr. Beckett and Julia Richards searched everywhere. At least, they searched until Julia collapsed in a fit of hysterics. Dr. Beckett got help from the townspeople. Scores of folk arrived and searched every inch of Charles' land. Some even began to dig up the ground where Charles had disappeared, in the belief that he'd fallen into a sinkhole or underground cavern and was even then trapped below. But it was solid ground. Charles was gone. He had disappeared in the full view of five people."

Jeff swallowed hard. "That's not the end of it. Tell me that's not the end."

"It's not," Malcolm said. "Weeks went by and the investigation ceased for lack of any clues. Julia, Dr. Beckett, the children, the young boy, they all testified again and again about what they'd seen. And there was no explanation for it.

"Julia was bedridden for months, lost in the hope that her husband would return. They never had a funeral or a memorial service. Eventually, a year later, they sold the farm and moved away."

Jeff jumped out of his chair. "That's it? That's the end of the story? What are you trying to do to me, Malcolm? You made that up!"

"No, Jeff. It's fully documented. Not only do I have the written testimonies of everyone who was there, but I managed to get tape recordings of the witnesses. Do you want to hear them?"

"No!" Jeff shouted. "You hear stories like this all the time. We don't know those people. Maybe they were up to something. Maybe they were in cahoots to get Richards' money!"

"Calm down," Malcolm said. "I can assure you that they were not."

"Yeah? How do you know? How can anyone know?"

"Because *I* was the young boy in the car. I worked with Dr. Beckett that summer. I saw it with my own eyes."

Jeff froze, staring in disbelief at his cousin. "But you're from England."

"As a lad — and a member of the Dubbs family — I sometimes came to Fawlt Line for my summer holidays. Your father and I became very close as a result. But after that incident, and my fascination with it, my parents stopped allowing those visits, to my deep regret."

Jeff thought about this for a moment, then said, "I still don't get it. What's your point?"

"My point is that there are a lot of things in heaven and on earth that are beyond our comprehension. If you and the Fordes are telling the truth about Elizabeth's disappearance, then it's entirely possible that she went the way of Charles Richards. Don't you see? I've been waiting for years for an event like this to happen again. I knew it would. Particularly in Fawlt Line."

Jeff looked helplessly at Malcolm. There was no way to measure his love for the man, but this was too much to be believed. "That's your theory? You think that the people of Fawlt Line don't just disappear like normal people, but they disappear to ... to *where*?"

"I don't know. But I have another theory."

"Another. Is it as bad as the first one?"

"Yes — if you mean by 'bad' that it's difficult to believe."

"You can define it that way if you want."

Malcolm paused as if unsure about continuing. Then he took a deep breath and said, "I went to Washington to meet with a doctor friend of mine who has been studying phenomena like the story I just told you. Jeff, there are so many things we don't know or understand about time and space. But my friend's research gives strong indications that there's more going on than most of us are willing to grasp."

"Uh oh. Here come the aliens," Jeff said.

"Not quite, but I want you to think about dreams for a moment."

"Dreams?"

Malcolm nodded. "I'm also interested in somnambulistic phenomena."

"Somnambulistic," Jeff repeated. "Sounds like an underwater emergency vehicle."

Malcolm smiled. "It means sleepwalking, but I see it as something bigger. I'm interested in dreams ... the subconscious — and how they connect to the unexplainable, like the sudden disappearances. Now, what if there is a point of entry into another time or dimension of space ... through a dream? What if things we often dismiss because we think they're simply part of the imagination or a so-called dream are truly a — how can I say it? — a *glimpse* into an alternative reality or time? What if, somehow, the brain crosses over and takes a peek at what's there? And *that's* what we're seeing?"

Stuck for an answer, Jeff could only look quizzically at his cousin.

Malcolm spread his hands. "And if the brain can do it, why not an entire body? Are you with me? That's what we're studying. We're suggesting that the mysterious disappearances of some of these people throughout history may mean that there's a *physical* point of entry between our world and whatever that other world is."

"But how?" Jeff asked. "How do you and your doctor friend think people physically jump from one world to the other?"

Malcolm sighed. "We don't know."

"So you're saying that Elizabeth sort of fell asleep in the bathtub and then slipped over to another world somewhere?"

Malcolm smiled sheepishly and shrugged.

Jeff wanted to believe him. He was desperate to believe that Elizabeth was safe and sound somewhere, even if that somewhere was somewhere impossible. But he *couldn't* believe it. "Malcolm?"

"Yes, Jeff?"

"If I were you, I wouldn't mention your theory to anybody else."

15

Elizabeth's day at the hospital was filled with daytime television programs she didn't recognize, but which were still awful; a casual chat with Dr. Waite who was pleased about her "decision" to work at being Sarah; and another round of therapy with the group. This time the old man had amended his memories of being bombed out in the Blitz to being a cook on a ship in the South Seas. Dr. Waite suggested that Elizabeth treat her memories like "a very realistic dream" and embrace Sarah's life in the here and now.

At dinnertime, the nurse didn't come with her food. She was just about to buzz for it when Calvin arrived in a nice suit and tie, announcing that he had Dr. Waite's permission to take her out for the evening. Elizabeth was pleased, if only at the opportunity to get away from the hospital for a while, but realized that she didn't have any clothes to wear.

"I can't go out dressed like this," she said.

With a wave of his hand, Calvin stepped into the hall and returned with a couple of outfits he'd picked from Sarah's closet. *"Voila!"*

While Calvin waited in the hall, Elizabeth quickly made her choice and slipped into a dress. It fit perfectly. Shaking off a gathering feeling of melancholy, she opened the door for Calvin, who rewarded her with a whistle and an approving smile.

They walked to Giovanni's, an Italian restaurant only two blocks from the hospital. "Doctor's orders," Calvin said as they sat at their table. "I can't take you too far — yet."

Elizabeth looked around at the cloth-covered tables, the formally dressed waiters, paintings, and more silverware than she knew how to use. She grinned to herself. *Jeff would be lost in a place like this.*

"So, what do we talk about?" Calvin asked after their fettuccine and manicotti arrived. "Should I pretend you're a new arrival to town? Or maybe I should treat this like our very first date. Do you remember? You grilled me about my goals in life."

"Did I?"

"Yeah." He chuckled. "I felt like I was being interviewed. But that's the way you are. A no-nonsense kind of girl. You weren't about to hook up with a loser."

Elizabeth put down her fork. "You make me sound like a mercenary."

Calvin shrugged. "You're a girl who knows what she wants. Nothing wrong with that."

Elizabeth considered the phrase. Wasn't it really a nice way of saying that Sarah was self-serving? "Go on," she said.

"Let's see ... you know, er, knew I'm a senior in high school, hoping to get a scholarship to the U, and I'm doing a student internship at the bank."

"You want to be a banker?" Elizabeth said in surprise. "Bankers are supposed to be wimpy little guys with glasses. You won't qualify."

Calvin laughed. "Thank you. But I don't really plan to be a banker. I want to work in investments. I'm going to study business in college."

"Is that what you're really interested in?"

"I'm being practical. Trends and technology come and go, but we'll always need people who know about money." He pushed his fettuccine around for a moment, then gave her a tender look.

"You've encouraged me a lot. You helped me understand where my strengths are."

"Oh, so suddenly I'm a saint." Elizabeth laughed.

"Saint Sarah."

"Patron Saint of the Forlorn and Forgotten," Elizabeth continued, then stopped. That wasn't so funny.

Calvin lifted his Coke to her. "Or Patron Saint of the Newly Remembered."

The moment was recovered, and she lifted her glass of water.

"To the future," he said softly.

She gazed at him, then sighed and put her glass down.

"Sorry," he said.

She shook her head. "You don't have to apologize. You've been very, very nice to me and . . . I'm so confused."

Calvin reached across the table and gently placed his hand on hers. "No pressure," he said. "I guess I'm relieved to be here with you. We've had a hard time lately and — well, it's nice to have you back, even though you're not all the way back. If you know what I mean."

Elizabeth smiled noncommittally. The waiter brought their dessert and, for a while, they were distracted by the delicious taste. Calvin told her more about things they had done together. It created a picture for her of two very happy people. With money too. She wondered where all the money came from, but she didn't inquire. Her parents had always said it was rude to ask about things like that.

Hesitantly Elizabeth ventured back to their previous conversation. "Calvin, it sounds like we were having the time of our lives. So why were we having problems?"

He hedged. "If you don't remember, why go into it? It's over now."

"But — "

"We can have a new beginning," he said brightly. "I don't want to be insensitive, but, in a lot of ways, what's happened to you is good. I mean, I know it's tough for *you*, but it's kind of a blessing for *us*."

"I still don't understand. What kind of problems were we having that — "

"Forget it," he said sharply. "That was before. What's important is where we are right now."

His rebuke unsettled her. The entire conversation was troublesome. It compounded her feeling that she was an actress who had suddenly stepped into someone else's play. Too many questions and not enough answers.

He noticed her withdrawal. "I'm sorry. I didn't mean to get so irritated," he said.

"It's my fault. I just can't get it right. It's ... too much. I think we'd better go."

Calvin nodded, waved at a waiter for the bill, and they left. In front of the restaurant, Elizabeth shivered, then breathed in the cool evening air. The dusk cast a metallic blue light over the street. The restaurant's neon light buzzed overhead.

"The hospital is that way," he said, hooking his hand in her arm.

She hesitated. "Calvin, thank you very much for the dinner."

"You're welcome."

"But please don't take this the wrong way," she said carefully. "Would you mind if I walked back to the hospital alone?"

Calvin's jaw clenched. "I blew it. I pushed too hard, right? I'm sorry."

Elizabeth patted his hand as she slipped her arm away. "No. I'd just like to be alone for a little while. It's beautiful tonight, and I think it would do me a lot of good to walk back by myself."

"I'm not sure Dr. Waite would approve," Calvin said with a forced lightheartedness.

"He doesn't have to know. And I promise not to run away."

She reached up and kissed him lightly on the cheek. It seemed like the correct thing to do. "Thank you, Calvin."

He shoved his hands into his pockets. "Goodnight."

She walked away, glancing back once to see him still standing there under the green cursive Giovanni sign, glowering like a little kid who'd been left behind while his friends went on vacation.

Her emotions battled against each other as she walked. *Calvin is certainly charming. I can see why Sarah went for him. But what went wrong between them?* It made sense that Calvin wouldn't want to burden her with past conflicts, but was there *more* he wasn't saying for other reasons?

Elizabeth realized how vulnerable she was. People could tell her anything about themselves — or about Sarah — and she'd be inclined to believe them. How would she know any better? She was never the kind of girl to second-guess people's motives. But in this situation, was that smart thinking? Maybe she should be more careful. Maybe she shouldn't be so quick to trust everyone.

Her thoughts of vulnerability and trust made her remember that she didn't know if this part of town was safe. The offices on the street were dark, the shops closed. The sidewalk was empty, and only one car and a taxi passed by. Surely Calvin wouldn't have let her walk back to the hospital if it was a bad area of town. But she'd been so adamant about going alone — maybe he didn't want to be bossy.

She looked around and was relieved to see the hospital just a couple of blocks ahead at the end of the street.

Then she was grabbed and pulled into an alley.

16

Jeff had fallen asleep in front of the television. His sleep was fitful as he dreamt that he was waiting for hours at the Old Saw Mill for Elizabeth.

I'm in the corner facing the door . . . Elizabeth walks in . . . she sees me, she approaches slowly, reaching up to put her arms around my neck . . . I pull her close to kiss her . . . Then she steps back, and I look into her face . . . But it isn't her face . . . It's hardly a face at all . . . It's a skeletal blob with sunken eyes and rotting skin . . . I open my mouth to scream, but nothing comes out except a shrill ringing . . .

It was the phone.

Jeff grabbed it and realized too late that he was sweating and breathing heavily. "Hello?" he panted.

"Jeff? Hi, it's Jerry Anderson from the *Gazette*."

Just then the doorbell rang.

"I want to get a statement from you — and your cousin if he's around."

"Statement?" Jeff asked. "Statement about what?"

The doorbell rang again. *Mrs. Packer must be out*, Jeff thought. Then he heard the click of Malcolm's heels against the tiled floor in the front hallway.

"About Elizabeth," Jerry said, then stammered, "Uh, you have heard, haven't you?"

"Heard what?" Jeff asked.

The phone line was suddenly filled with the silence of Jerry's embarrassment. "Maybe I should talk to your cousin first."

Malcolm opened the front door, and Jeff could hear low voices. He was sure that one of them belonged to Sheriff Hounslow.

Something terrible has happened.

"Jeff?" Jerry Anderson said, his voice fading as Jeff slowly lowered the phone to his side and stared at the doorway of the room. Malcolm stood there with Sheriff Hounslow and another policeman.

"Jeff," Malcolm said. "We need to go to the hospital."

"Hello?" Jerry Anderson called again in a thin voice.

Jeff swallowed hard. "What's wrong?"

Malcolm looked at Jeff solemnly. "They found Elizabeth. She's in a coma."

17

In the alley, a rough hand clasped over her mouth.

"Don't scream," said a man's voice. "I'm not going to hurt you."

Elizabeth struggled anyway.

The man tightened his grip and pulled her into the shadows against the rough brick wall. He spoke quickly. "Listen to me. You're being followed by someone. Now just stay still until we can figure out who it is and whether you're safe or not, okay?"

His grip was strong enough to make Elizabeth realize that she couldn't overpower her captor. She relaxed a little and let her mind work out a way to escape.

He kept a firm hold on her but said nothing more. Both of them were breathing heavily. They faced the street where Elizabeth had just been walking. Rapid footsteps announced someone's approach. Suddenly, framed by the edge of the two buildings at the end of the alley, Calvin appeared. Elizabeth wanted to cry out, but knew better than to try it. Calvin looked around quickly, then moved on.

"Was he supposed to be following you?" the man asked. "'Cause I'll be honest. The way he was sneaking around behind you had me pretty worried."

Had you worried? Elizabeth thought. *You drag me into an alley with your hand over my mouth, and you're worried?*

"Let me explain," he said quickly. "I work for the hospital. I saw you in Dr. Waite's therapy group."

Oh no. I've been grabbed by one of the whackos.

As if he could read her mind, he said, "I'm not *in* the group. I just saw you there. I heard what you said — your story about being someone else. I wanted to talk to you because I understand how you feel. Maybe I can help you."

Her heart beat like a scared rabbit's. She didn't offer a response.

"Look," he said. "I'm going to let you go, and what I'd *like* to do is walk you back to the hospital. Will you let me do that? I'm not out to hurt you. Trust me."

Do I have a choice? she wondered. Then, figuring that cooperation might at least give her a chance to escape, she nodded her head.

Slowly he let go of her, but she was aware that his arms were ready to grab her again if she made a quick move. She turned to face him.

It was the hospital maintenance man.

"It's you," she said.

He seemed surprised. "You recognize me?"

"I saw you. You came into my first therapy meeting to clean up those dirty cups," she said. "What are you trying to pull? You scared me to death."

He hung his head repentantly. "I'm sorry. But I figured if I didn't get you fast, that guy might grab you."

"That *guy* is my boyfriend," Elizabeth snapped, then realized what she had said. "Well, he sort of is."

The man cocked an eyebrow. "What kind of boyfriend sneaks around like that? He sure didn't want you to know he was back there."

Elizabeth frowned. "Yeah? And why were you following me?"

"I've been trying to keep an eye on you ever since I heard your story," he said. "When I found out you left the hospital tonight, I was a little worried."

"Why? What do you care about me?"

"I care because ..." He paused. "Can we get out of this alley?"

"Good idea," she said. They walked to the end of the alley, checked to see if the sidewalk was clear, then stepped out and headed for the hospital. "I wish you'd just slipped me a note or something. My heart's about to pound out of my chest."

"Mine too." He smiled. "I don't normally grab young girls in the street."

"Glad to hear it," she said, and then reminded herself that she wasn't supposed to trust people so willingly. "Okay, finish what you were saying. Why do you care what happens to me?"

"Well, I took a peek at your hospital records, and I don't believe you're a fruitcake."

"Thank you."

"Which means that you're telling the truth when you talk about not being from here — that you *do* have another life, the one you remember."

"So?"

"So, I'm here to tell you that you need to believe in those memories. They're real. Don't you let anyone tell you differently."

Elizabeth felt divided. Part of her wanted to cry from the relief that someone believed her, another part was angry, defensive. "How do you know that?" she demanded.

"Because the same thing happened to me."

Elizabeth stopped in her tracks. "What?"

"I won't get into the whole story right now. But one day I showed up here and everybody kept calling me one name, and I kept saying I had another name, that I was another person, and just like you, they treated me like some kind of amnesiac. Time and persistence finally made me give in. I thought, 'Hey, if calling me George will help us get along, then I'll be George.'

I've been George for a long, long time. So, do I call you Sarah or Elizabeth?"

Elizabeth scrunched her face up with indecision. "I haven't been here a long, long time." She gestured toward the hospital. "They think I'm Sarah, and I'm starting to believe them. So that's who I say I am. It doesn't make any sense. But I'm gonna be honest: I don't know if I should believe a word you're saying."

George chuckled low and long. "I don't blame you — especially after listening to all those stories from the folks in your therapy group. What can I say to convince you I'm not nuts?"

"I don't know if you can say anything to convince me," Elizabeth admitted. "For all I know, you're as much a dream as everything else. But I'd sure like to know how I got here if I don't really belong here."

George scratched his temple. "I've been thinking about it for years, and I'm still not sure. I have an idea though."

"Go ahead."

"First: how's your belief?" he asked.

"My belief in what?"

He smiled. "Your belief in things you can't see, things that are too bizarre for us to understand."

Elizabeth thought about her parents and their small-part-of-a-bigger-picture lectures. It was all connected to going to church, she knew, but she couldn't be sure how. She shrugged as an answer.

"That'll have to do, I guess," George said. He hesitated. "I figure that we're from an alternative time, and somehow we got crossed-over to this time." He glanced at her warily.

She sighed. "I'm not a big science fiction fan. You wanna tell me how that's possible?"

"I don't know," George confessed. "As best as I can figure, it's like switching channels on the TV. You know how sometimes if you catch two programs at the right moment, they seem to belong together? A character on channel two will say 'How are you?' and, if you switch to channel three, a character on another program says 'I'm fine, thanks.' Maybe it's like that."

"That's just a coincidence, though," Elizabeth argued.

"I'm a big believer in coincidences. They're the secret workings of God. You do believe in God, don't you?"

"Well ..."

"It doesn't matter. He's working whether you believe in Him or not." By now they'd reached a side entrance to the hospital. He opened the large metal door for her.

Elizabeth thought again of her parents, of their persistent faith in God and in a reality that went beyond her own. Did she really believe it?

"You think it was a coincidence that we met? It wasn't," he said.

She eyed him uneasily. He didn't seem crazy, but how much was she expected to believe? "This is really hard to swallow. I mean, it's easier to believe that I'm just Sarah who lost her memory."

"I know, I know." George nodded sympathetically. "You have to hang on. Keep faith in the truth. I'll help you if I can. But we have to stick together."

He stepped back outside and closed the door behind him, leaving her in an empty stairwell. She wasn't sure what to think. On the one hand, she was relieved to hear that someone understood how she felt. On the other hand, she couldn't help but be alarmed that someone else was crazy enough to understand! *She* certainly wouldn't understand, if it hadn't happened to her.

"Stick together," she whispered, her voice a soft hiss in the echo around her. "I'm not sure I like that idea."

18

Jeff raced into the hospital room, but was pulled back like a reined-in horse by Malcolm's firm hand on his shoulder. From the door he saw Alan and Jane Forde by the bed. A nurse was at the head, adjusting pillows. They all looked up at him as if they thought he might be a doctor with news. Alan rose to his feet but didn't speak. Malcolm gave Jeff a gentle nudge forward.

His legs felt rubbery and his shoes were like concrete slabs as he walked to the side of the bed and looked down at the figure lying there.

It was Elizabeth. She looked emaciated, her pale face stark against the white hospital gown. Her breathing was harsh and strained.

Jeff gritted his teeth to fight back the sorrow. The nurse pulled the sheet up as if tucking her in for a quiet night's sleep.

"She was found half-immersed in the river, close to the Old Saw Mill," Sheriff Hounslow said from somewhere behind them.

Mrs. Forde sobbed. She was clinging to a bundle in her lap. It looked to Jeff like black sweatpants, and draped over her knees was a T-shirt with a graphic design on it.

Jeff turned his eyes to Elizabeth again. Her hair was matted, and there were dark circles under her eyes. Her throat was bruised and puffy. *What happened to you, Bits?*

Alan Forde began to whisper a prayer. Malcolm tapped Jeff on the shoulder and gestured for him to come out into the hall.

Hounslow was already there. He moved away from the doorway, speaking quietly as Malcolm and Jeff followed. "She was found by some kids who were looking for a new fishing spot. She was partially hidden beneath an overgrowth of bushes along the edge. The current probably took her there. The searchers didn't find her because the bushes obscured everything unless you looked from just the right angle."

"What did the doctor say?" Malcolm asked.

"He figures someone tried to strangle her, then dumped her into the river." Sheriff Hounslow dropped some coins into a coffee vending machine. "Maybe the attacker thought she was dead. Maybe he or she was interrupted. We don't know."

"Were there any other signs of physical violence?" Malcolm asked carefully.

The sheriff shook his head. "No. She was choked, nothing else. But she's in pretty bad shape. Doc is running tests — and wants to run more. He can't tell yet if there's any brain activity or not."

Jeff's heart broke. He struggled to fight the burning in his eyes. "Who did it? Any ideas?"

The coffee machine gurgled and clicked as it poured Sheriff Hounslow his cup of coffee. "No," he answered, then scrutinized Jeff's face. "Do *you* have any ideas?"

The question was full of suspicion, and Jeff knew right away that he was still a suspect.

"We want you to come to the station for questioning," Hounslow said. The walkie-talkie on his belt came to life in a sudden burst of static. The sheriff excused himself, grabbed his coffee, and ventured to the waiting room to talk to one of his officers.

"Don't worry," Malcolm said softly.

"I want to go back into the room to be with Elizabeth."

In the room, Malcolm and Jeff sat next to Elizabeth's parents.

They didn't speak. After a moment Jane clasped Jeff's hand tightly, so tightly it trembled. Jeff glanced away, his eye falling on the T-shirt that was still draped like a flag over Jane's knee. He saw the artwork more clearly. *The Montfair Rock & Jazz Festival, August 12 – 15th*, it said.

Sheriff Hounslow appeared in the room and looked expectantly at Jeff. He and Malcolm exchanged looks, and they both followed the sheriff out of the room and down to the police station.

———

"They think I tried to kill her!" Jeff said as he and Malcolm drove away from the station two hours later. Night had fallen, and a bright moon shone down on them.

"Let them think what they want," Malcolm said calmly. "Unless they have solid evidence, they can't do anything but ask you questions."

"But why — " Jeff lamented, "*why* would they think — I mean, *how* could they think I'd do that to Elizabeth? I love her!" The words were out before he could stop himself.

Malcolm looked over at Jeff. "Is that so?"

"You know I do," Jeff said.

"Well, I always suspected you did. I was waiting for you to figure it out."

They drove on silently.

Jeff could tell from Malcolm's expression that he was thinking through their situation. "Sheriff Hounslow is focusing on the argument you had in the diner," Malcolm eventually said.

"It wasn't really an argument. I was trying to talk her out of running away."

"That's what you say. But all anyone else knows is that you were arguing," Malcolm said. "Hounslow is simply drawing what seems to him to be a logical conclusion. You met Elizabeth at the Old Saw Mill down by the river, the argument continued, things got out of control. In a fit of anger you grabbed her, strangled her, and threw her body into the river in panic."

"But I'd never lay a hand on her. Ever!" Jeff said. "Not even when we were kidding around."

Malcolm nodded. "Everyone who knows you doesn't doubt that for a minute. But Hounslow doesn't know you. And even if he did, Jeff, it's his responsibility to consider all the possibilities."

They drove on in silence for another mile.

Malcolm sighed deeply, his brow furrowed.

"What's wrong?" Jeff asked.

"It still doesn't make sense," he said. "How did she get from a locked bathroom — with no escape — to the Old Saw Mill?"

19

Morning arrived and with it Dr. Waite. Elizabeth had just finished tying her shoes when he walked in clutching his clipboard like a life preserver. He smiled, but didn't say anything. Elizabeth looked at him, perplexed. Still he didn't speak. He just stood looking like the cat that swallowed the canary.

Elizabeth put her hands on her hips and stared at him. "Okay, I give up," she finally said.

"You can go home."

"Home?"

"I'm persuaded that you are ready to leave the hospital," he said. "I believe you've made enough progress — not a lot, mind you, but sufficient enough to release you. Getting out of here will probably aid your recovery, particularly once you're back in your old surroundings."

Which old surroundings? she wanted to ask, but she checked the thought.

"Of course, I'll expect you to continue coming to our therapy meetings," he added. "We have a lot left to sort through."

She nodded noncommittally and remembered her encounter with George last night. *Now* there's *somebody for the therapy group*, she thought.

Calvin's head appeared around the corner. "Well?" he said, wearing a sheepish smile.

"Get her out of here," Dr. Waite said playfully. In a flurry of his white smock, he was gone.

"Get packed and I'll take you home," Calvin said.

Elizabeth wasn't sure. "You mean *your* home, right?"

"You don't have any other, do you?"

"But ... are you really sure you ...? I mean ..." She wasn't certain what she meant. Maybe her uneasiness was born out of not wanting to be an imposition. Maybe it was because she didn't want to go back with Calvin to his iceberg parents.

Calvin streamed past her toward her suitcase. "Don't be stupid. Pack up and let's get out of here."

The drive through Fawlt Line gave her the creeps. Once again she was able to see the marked similarities and differences from the town she remembered. She closed her eyes tight and opened them again, hoping that one reality or the other would take hold. If she were Elizabeth, she wanted to be *completely* Elizabeth. If she were Sarah, then God, please let her be Sarah. Just one or the other. Was it so much to ask?

"How was your walk back to the hospital last night?" Calvin asked abruptly as they passed the old McIntyre's Lumber store. In *her* Fawlt Line, it had a giant plastic lumberjack on the roof; this one didn't.

"Okay," she said. "I was nervous when I realized I didn't know how safe the neighborhood was." She quickly decided that telling him about George wouldn't help anything. Calvin would probably get the poor man fired.

Calvin persisted, his voice strained. "Did you see anyone?"

"That's a funny question," Elizabeth said as she turned her face away, looking out the window. "Why do you ask?"

"Because I saw you with someone," he said sharply. "The two of you went in the side entrance to the hospital."

"That was just someone who works at the hospital. He opened the door for me," Elizabeth said, then pivoted in the seat to face him. "Were you following me?"

Calvin's knuckles were white around the steering wheel. "I was worried. I wanted to make sure you got back safe."

"How kind of you," she said sarcastically, bothered at this clear display of his jealousy.

He glanced at her. "Well? Who is this new chum, huh?"

Elizabeth folded her arms defiantly. "It's a worker at the hospital. That's all."

He growled as he took the curb onto the driveway too hard. Elizabeth nearly fell into him. Calvin brought the car to a stop, yanked the keys from the ignition, and got out. He slammed the door and stormed up to the house, leaving her to get her suitcase. Elizabeth anxiously watched him. Why the sudden jealous outburst? He'd been so charming until now. It didn't match up. But what did she know for sure? How could she know anyone in just a couple of days? *I shouldn't be so trusting*, she thought as she got out of the car. She pulled her case from the back seat and carried it up to Sarah's room.

She had just put the clothes away when there was a gentle tap on the door.

"Come in," she said.

Calvin peeked in, looking contrite. "I'm sorry," he said. "I don't know why I acted like that."

"I don't know either." She shoved the empty suitcase into the bottom of the closet.

"A lot has happened," he explained. "I feel really stressed. I'm sorry. Can you forgive me?"

Saying sorry was one thing; asking for forgiveness was another. Elizabeth had been raised to believe it was the deepest kind of apology a person could make. "Never mind," she said, smiling faintly. "You've been so nice to me. I'm sorry I upset you."

He smiled back at her. "Really? Do you mean it?"

"Of course."

He lingered for a moment, watching her. "You are different, you know."

"I am?"

"The old Sarah never apologized for anything."

She blushed and began busying herself with the clothes in the closet.

"Sarah," Calvin said.

Elizabeth turned.

He smiled proudly. "You see? You *are* Sarah."

Elizabeth looked away and in her own mind conceded that small victory to him. *It's so much easier this way*, she thought as she remembered that crazy George guy's remark about answering to the new name. *It sure beats being treated like a lunatic.*

———

Later, while Calvin was busy washing his car, Elizabeth dug a phone number out of her jeans pocket and slipped to the phone in the kitchen. Calvin's parents were still at work. She picked up the receiver and dialed a number. Rhonda answered.

"It's Eli — I mean, it's Sarah. I'm out of the hospital and back at Calvin's. You said to call if I ever wanted to get out for a while. Well, I'm calling."

Rhonda said she was just on her way out to do some shopping and would be happy to pick her up.

Outside on the porch, Calvin worked unsuccessfully to mask his annoyance when she told him where she was going. "This isn't a good idea," he complained. "Dr. Waite would be against it."

"Do you want me to call him and ask?" Elizabeth offered.

"No," he said. "But you don't remember how Rhonda is."

"How is Rhonda?" Elizabeth asked, wondering again what she may have been dropped into with the complexities of Sarah's life and her friends.

"You two aren't good for each other," he said. "She was always a bad influence on you."

"How could I know that?" Elizabeth asked.

Calvin's face took on the same expression he'd had when he was angry in the car, but this time he kept the emotion in check. He groaned, throwing up his hands. "I give up. Have fun," he said through taut lips.

Rhonda arrived ten minutes later, and Elizabeth jumped into the passenger side of her small economy car. Somehow it seemed an odd match for Rhonda's sports-car personality. She was a beautiful girl with short hair and an athletic build.

The girls chatted about Elizabeth's release from the hospital, Dr. Waite — mostly chitchat to fill the time until they arrived at Darcy Street, a main road in town dedicated to shops of all kinds. Elizabeth felt envious. Her Fawlt Line didn't have that kind of shopping district.

Once they'd parked, Rhonda dragged her into a particularly expensive boutique. They looked over a rack of blouses and Rhonda said, "So, tell me what really happened in the hospital. Did they stick you with a bunch of lunatics?"

Elizabeth laughed. "Technically speaking, I'm one of those lunatics, you know."

"You're no lunatic," Rhonda said. "A problem child, maybe, but no lunatic. Now tell me everything that happened to you there."

Elizabeth hesitated, knowing she had to make a choice about whether or not to trust this old friend of Sarah's who was a new friend to her. She decided she must, if only to learn more about what she — or Sarah — really was like. She told her about the therapy group and how she'd spent her time, and included her dinner with Calvin and the walk back to the hospital.

"Did you see anyone else at the hospital?" Rhonda asked.

"No," Elizabeth replied, wondering if Rhonda somehow knew about Crazy George. "Who else would I have seen?"

Rhonda glanced up at her. "Lots of people might have

dropped by to see you. Why do you sound as if you're guilty of something?"

Elizabeth pushed a group of blouses around the rack. "Because Calvin asked me the same question and got really mad." It was all she could think to say.

Rhonda rolled her eyes. "Oh, not that again."

Elizabeth looked blank. "Not what again?"

Rhonda took a sharp breath. "Look, I don't want to cause problems while you two are trying to repair your relationship."

"Why does our relationship need to be repaired?" Elizabeth asked. "I'm the amnesiac around here. I don't know anything."

Rhonda gazed at her, making a decision. Finally she said, "Calvin's really possessive. It used to drive you nuts." She hesitated. "But maybe the *new* you won't mind it."

"I don't know what I like. I'm having a hard time thinking of him as a boyfriend, when he's a stranger to me," Elizabeth said, then held up a fashionable blouse. "Would the old me wear this?"

Rhonda frowned and shook her head. "Not in a million years. But if you like it, get it. There are no rules about who you have to be, right? I mean, how many of us get a chance to completely reinvent ourselves?"

Elizabeth thought that was an interesting way to look at it. If she could figure out how to get some money, maybe she'd buy some new clothes.

"So nobody else visited you?" Rhonda asked a little too casually.

"That's the second time you've asked me that," Elizabeth said. "You have someone particular in mind."

Rhonda looked coy and shrugged.

"Come on," Elizabeth coaxed her. "Who are you thinking about?"

"You won't remember anyway."

"Then it won't matter if you tell me," Elizabeth reasoned.

Rhonda couldn't argue, so she said simply, "David. I thought David would come to see you."

The name meant nothing to Elizabeth. "Sorry. I'm blank about David. Who is he?"

Rhonda smiled mischievously. "No comment."

"No fair."

"Honest," she said. "You're better off leaving some things alone — and he's one of them."

Elizabeth wanted to ask more, but decided that a new character in this strange play would only complicate things. Maybe she'd ask again later. Much later.

They spent the rest of the afternoon shopping. Elizabeth got the feeling that it was a ritual — a test — to see if Rhonda and the "new" Sarah could be friends as they were before. For Elizabeth, the answer was yes. She liked Rhonda. There was something "big city" about her, unlike the girlfriends she was used to in her old Fawlt Line.

But after Rhonda dropped her off at Calvin's house that evening, Elizabeth reflected on their conversation about who else she had seen at the hospital. Had Calvin also been wondering if she had seen this mysterious David? Or was it just a coincidence?

Coincidences, Elizabeth could hear Crazy George say, *are the secret workings of God.*

She walked up the dusk-lit driveway and looked at the silhouette of Calvin's somber, foreboding house. It sent a chill down her spine.

20

Jeff paced from one end of Elizabeth's hospital room to the other, accompanied by the rhythmic hiss and blip of the equipment connected to the comatose girl.

Mr. and Mrs. Forde had gone to get dinner in the hospital cafeteria. They wouldn't be away long, Jeff knew. They had suspended their lives to stay near their daughter.

A police officer, assigned to guard Elizabeth from whoever hurt her in the first place, watched Jeff warily from the doorway.

Wake up, Bits, Jeff prayed. *Come on, you can do it.* He took to counting backward from ten, like a rocket countdown, hoping she'd open her eyes when he got to one. *Lift off.*

But she lay in the same solemn state she had been in since they brought her from the river.

Jeff's eye caught sight of the closet door — open slightly — the hangers sitting empty in the narrow light. He thought again about the T-shirt Elizabeth's mother had been holding. He tried to remember the artwork on the front. It advertised some sort of music festival. It struck Jeff now that it was a shirt he'd never seen Elizabeth wear before.

A cleared throat sounded from behind him. Jeff spun around. Sheriff Hounslow stood at the edge of Elizabeth's bed.

"No change, huh?" he said.

Jeff shook his head.

"Come on out into the hall," the sheriff said. "I want to ask you a couple of questions."

Jeff didn't move. "I don't think Malcolm wants me to answer any more of your questions unless he's here."

"It's routine stuff, Jeff. Look, the more I learn, the less I'm inclined to think that you had anything to do with this. Just a couple of questions, that's all. Help me out, will you? Besides, your cousin isn't even in town."

That was true. Malcolm had flown back to Washington, D.C., for reasons he didn't explain to Jeff.

Reluctantly, Jeff stepped into the hall with the law officer.

Hounslow popped a piece of chewing gum into his mouth. "Let me get this straight. You said you went into the Old Saw Mill and didn't leave until we found you, right?"

"Right."

"Then why did we find your footprints along the river's edge?"

The question took Jeff back as his memory searched for an answer. "I don't know."

"And what about the fingerprints we found?"

"What were they on?"

"An iron rod."

Jeff remembered. "I was bored while I waited. So I went down to the river. The rod was lying there. I picked it up and threw it into the bushes."

Sheriff Hounslow chewed his gum noisily, his jaw working like a machine. "Why didn't you say so before?"

"I didn't think about it before," Jeff answered.

"So you went down to the river," he mused. "But your footprints were up and down that part of the river's edge, like you were running. Why?"

"I thought I heard a car pull into another part of the saw mill. So I ran up to see if it might be Elizabeth. No one was there, so

I ran back." Even as Jeff spoke, he knew it sounded feeble. He braced himself.

Hounslow merely offered a stiff nod. "Okay. That's all."

Jeff was relieved. Could it really be that simple? He felt brave enough to speak. "Now I have a question for you," Jeff said.

Hounslow cocked an eyebrow at him.

"What happened to Elizabeth's clothes? The ones she was wearing when she was found."

"They're being looked over for forensic evidence. Why?"

"The T-shirt," Jeff said. "Do you remember what was on it? It had some kind of artwork."

Hounslow pulled a notepad out of his back pocket and flipped it open. "Let's see. Black T-shirt with gold, cursive-style letters. 'The Montfair Rock & Jazz Festival, August 12–15.' Why?"

"I'm curious. I've never seen Elizabeth wear that shirt. I've never even heard of the Montfair Festival, have you?"

"No — and there's no reason I would," the sheriff said. He turned and, with a nod to the officer on duty, began to walk away.

The sheriff suddenly stopped and faced him again. "By the way, tell your cousin to hire that lawyer for you. You're gonna need one."

"What?" Jeff felt as if he'd been jabbed in the stomach.

"As I see it, we've got witnesses to your fight at the diner, your footprints and fingerprints were found at the river's edge only a few yards from where we think she was attacked, and that iron rod is being checked out as a possible weapon." He smiled triumphantly. "I'd arrest you now, but I kinda hope you'll try to run for it. That'll help us sway the jury, just in case they're undecided."

Jeff gaped at him.

Hounslow nodded toward Elizabeth's room. "And I don't need to tell you the mess you'll be in if that girl dies." He walked off.

Stunned, Jeff leaned against the cold hospital wall. The police officer by Elizabeth's door smirked at him. Jeff looked away. *This can't be happening.*

He pressed his fists against his eyes, trying to think. All the same questions ricocheted around in his head. *What happened to Elizabeth that night? How did she get out of a locked bathroom? Why would she wander in her sweatpants, T-shirt, and tennis shoes to the Old Saw Mill to meet me? If she was going to run away, why didn't she bring her suitcase and belongings?* Jeff glanced down the hall at the retreating figure of Sheriff Hounslow. *So many questions, and he's not even trying to answer them anymore. He's sure I did it.*

Without looking at the police officer, Jeff walked back into the room with its hissing and blips and stopped at the bed. He looked at Elizabeth's face, bruised and bloated, so lifeless. He imagined her at the river that night, wondering if he really had heard her drive up. What if she was in the clutches of her attacker, prevented from crying out, while Jeff stood only a few yards away? He bit his lower lip to stop the tears that wanted to come.

The car, he wondered. *Was there a car? How did she get from her house to the river? Might she have hitched a ride?*

He stared at the comatose form, imagining her in the sweatpants, T-shirt, and tennis shoes they'd found her in. Something was wrong with that picture. He thought about the T-shirt again. *The Montfair Rock and Jazz Festival.* He drew another blank. He'd never heard of it and had never seen her wear that shirt. So where did it come from?

It was worth investigating — a small mystery that might help with the bigger one. If he couldn't pray Elizabeth awake, maybe he could do something else to help.

First things first. Who would know how to find out about the festival?

Who else but Malcolm?

21

Waking up in a room that was like her own but really wasn't put Elizabeth in the doldrums again. At least in the hospital she could consent to being Sarah without really having to *be* Sarah. But here in Sarah's room — *her* room — she was face-to-face with reality. She couldn't escape. This was her life now.

Dr. Waite had instructed her to go through her bedroom thoroughly. Get acquainted with it. See if anything triggered her memory; a blouse bought for a special occasion, a knick-knack from a friend, a borrowed book, a report card or school paper, letters, photos, emails or other files on her computer. The smallest, seemingly insignificant item could open up her mind to Sarah's life. If nothing else, it was a way to make peace with who Sarah was as a means to unite the two people into one. How did Sarah decorate, what did she wear, where did she put things?

She turned on the computer, but was instantly thwarted when it asked for a password. She guessed at a couple, with no results, and gave up. So much for that.

A few moments in the closet convinced Elizabeth that Sarah didn't have very good taste in clothes. Elizabeth didn't like anything she saw.

Behind the clothes, Elizabeth found a box. She pulled it out and found the very things Dr. Waite had hoped she would find: keepsakes and paraphernalia of a life she didn't know. A small stack of report cards from Sarah's years at school. There were teacher's comments, consistent over each passing grade: Sarah was — is — quite artistic, but her organizational skills are atrocious. She is an average student.

There were birthday cards and notes from friends and girl-friends. One card was from Rhonda, laughing over a bit of mischief she and Sarah had gotten into. Another card from Calvin pleaded with Sarah to forgive him for some unspecified offense.

She found a book of drawings, including half-finished sketches of horses and landscapes and a fairly good likeness of Rhonda. *I'm pretty good*, Elizabeth said to herself.

A small blue book, jammed with bank statements, caught her attention. Elizabeth was momentarily impressed that Sarah even had a bank account … then she discovered that the account had over fifty thousand dollars in it. "Wow," Elizabeth gasped. Tucked into a pouch at the front of the book was a copy of a will. It was Sarah's parents' will, naming her as sole heir to all they owned, their insurance, everything — to the tune of more than seven hundred thousand dollars. "Wow!" she said again.

Elizabeth glanced through the pages and found a paragraph making it clear that she couldn't touch the money until she was eighteen. Meanwhile, she was to be placed under the guardianship of the executor of the estate or whomever he designates. According to the will, the guardians get a generous allowance for taking care of her.

Typed into the blank line for her designated guardians was "Ted and Barbara Collins" — Calvin's parents. Now she understood better why she was living there, and why they put up with her when they obviously disliked her.

She dropped the papers back into the box and pulled out a yellowed newspaper clipping wrapped in plastic. There, in an unfocused black-and-white photo and smudged type, was the chronicle of John and Kathryn Bishop's death in a car accident on Route 57. It was a straightforward incident. A rainy night, a slippery road, and a truck coming too fast in the opposite direction. The photo was an anniversary picture of John and Kathryn taken the year before they'd died. They didn't look at all like Alan and Jane Forde. Elizabeth was grateful for that. But it didn't take away the sudden and sickly feeling in her stomach.

Regardless of who she was — Elizabeth or Sarah — they both felt the loss. Her parents, whoever they were, were gone. If she was Sarah, they were dead from a car accident. If she was Elizabeth, they were still lost to her. Mere memories. She fell back against the wall, stung by the realization. Her parents were no longer part of her life.

Elizabeth thought about her desire to run away. It was a thoughtless, self-centered idea that didn't take into account how her mother and father might feel about losing her — or how she would feel without them. What was she thinking? She thought about Jeff, understanding the loss he must have felt when his parents had died.

How did he bear it? And how could she have been so insensitive?

Overwhelmed with her feeling of loss and shame, Elizabeth recklessly shoved the keepsakes back into the box. She argued with her emotions. *The parents I knew — even Jeff — are part of my overactive imagination. If I'm Sarah, then there is no Jeff to feel bad about. His parents couldn't have died because he doesn't exist, except in my mind. It's stupid to feel bad about imaginary characters.*

She told herself that she *must* be Sarah. How else could she cope? She'd lose her mind otherwise.

You win, Sarah, she thought as she turned to the dresser. *Elizabeth is the dream. You are the reality.* She rifled through the clothes that had been dropped haphazardly into the dresser drawers, and stopped to fold a few shirts and stack them neatly. *It's foolish to cling to misplaced memories*, she told herself.

I'm a girl named Sarah who hit her head on the side of the tub and suffered amnesia. I must start my life all over again.

Methodically, she worked her way from the top drawer to the bottom. She was Sarah, but a *changed* Sarah. Things would have to be different.

On her knees, she slid open the bottom drawer and pulled out the clothes. In the back, under some old white socks, she was surprised to find a Bible. *A Bible?* That wasn't consistent with the Sarah she was getting to know. She flipped it open and found an inscription to Sarah from Mrs. Skelton, her third-grade Sunday school teacher. Apart from the usual text, there were color illustrations of Bible stories: Moses with the Ten Commandments, David slaying Goliath, Elijah calling down fire from heaven on the priests of Baal, Jesus gathering children on his knee … Elizabeth turned the pages and found a pressed flower, brittle purple and black.

She leaned toward the closet, intending to put the Bible in the keepsake box later. She fumbled it and it fell to the floor. Papers that had been stuck in the back pages spilled out. One was a tattered baptismal certificate. The other was a white square, the backside of a photograph. It was face down and Elizabeth could see handwriting. "David — Veteran's Day Picnic" it said. The handwriting faintly resembled her own.

"David," she whispered, hopeful that she might finally see who this mysterious person was. She picked up the photo and turned it over.

It was a picture of a young man with curly black hair standing next to a tree, a mischievous smile on his face. Elizabeth gasped and dropped the photo like a curse, stepping back, her hand to her mouth, not believing what she had clearly seen and afraid to look at it again. But she did.

The young man in the photo was Jeff.

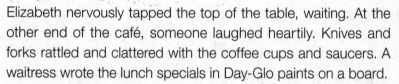

22

Elizabeth nervously tapped the top of the table, waiting. At the other end of the café, someone laughed heartily. Knives and forks rattled and clattered with the coffee cups and saucers. A waitress wrote the lunch specials in Day-Glo paints on a board.

Rhonda casually looked at the photograph of David, then back at Elizabeth. "Why are you showing this to me? I know what David looks like."

"But I don't — I mean, I didn't until this morning. Now I want to know everything about him."

Rhonda smiled impishly as she sipped her soda. "Why don't you ask Calvin? He'd have a few choice things to say about David."

Elizabeth frowned. "That's what I'm afraid of. That's why I'm asking you instead."

"Does Calvin know you're meeting me for lunch?"

"No, I didn't tell him. I don't have to tell him everything, do I?"

"You used to," Rhonda answered. "And it drove you crazy."

Elizabeth glanced across the room and saw someone who looked a lot like Calvin. It made her jump. It was true — she was instinctively afraid of Calvin's reaction, his jealousy, if he found she had sneaked out to have lunch with Rhonda to talk about David. Elizabeth leaned forward and spoke quietly. "Rhonda, I'm really confused. You're the only one I can count on."

"Yeah, sure," Rhonda said. Then she tossed her head back and laughed. "It's so funny to hear you say that. There were times when I didn't think you ever counted on *anyone*, Sarah."

"I'm different now."

Rhonda looked at Elizabeth, scrutinizing her. "I guess you are."

"So, tell me about David. It would mean a lot to me if I knew."

Rhonda ran her fingers through her short hair. It fell back into place perfectly and, for a second, Elizabeth wondered why she couldn't have hair like that. "How am I supposed to start? It's hard to launch into who David Wilcox is."

"I don't want his whole life story," Elizabeth said impatiently. "I just want to know what he has to do with *me*."

Rhonda shook her head. "No, Sarah. It's what he has to do with all of us. See, David was my boyfriend."

"*Your* boyfriend!" Elizabeth exclaimed. "Then why do I have his picture hidden away like that?"

Rhonda's lips slid into a razor-thin smile. "Because you met him through me when things were bad between you and Calvin. And you were nuts about him."

Elizabeth's mouth fell open. "I fell for *your* boyfriend?"

She nodded, the smile frozen in place. "And you finally got him."

"I *stole* him from you?" Elizabeth was aghast.

"That's one way of putting it," Rhonda said.

Elizabeth shook her head, blushing as she did. "You must have hated me."

"It put a strain on our relationship." Rhonda fiddled with the straw in her drink.

"So ..." Elizabeth began reluctantly. "What happened?"

"That's the mystery," Rhonda said, drawing herself up in her seat. "He was going to run away with you the night ... well, the night everything changed for you."

Elizabeth nearly knocked over her soda. "Run away?"

"Yeah. You said you had figured out a way to get to your inheritance, and you were gonna leave Fawlt Line for good. That's what I thought had happened, until I heard you were in the hospital with amnesia. That's why I wasn't sure about you. I figured you were up to another one of your old tricks."

Elizabeth put her face in her hands. The similarities between her story and Sarah's were too close to deny. If Dr. Waite was there, he'd say it was another link to show that the two of them really were the same person. "Where is David now?" she asked.

"He's around," Rhonda answered.

"Are you seeing him again?"

"Are you kidding? Not a chance," Rhonda replied.

"Will you help me?" Elizabeth asked. "Will you set it up so I can meet him?"

"Don't do it, Sarah. Forget about him. It could ruin everything all over again."

Elizabeth shook her head quickly. "No, you don't understand. I have to see him. I'll go crazy if I don't." She looked Rhonda directly in the eyes. "You have to help me. Or I'll find him some other way."

Rhonda leaned back in her seat and gazed at Elizabeth silently. Then she laughed — a cold, humorless laugh. "That's more like it. That's the Sarah I know."

"I don't care," Elizabeth said, undaunted. "I have to meet David. Not because I want to get back with him, but because it'll help my amnesia. Maybe something happened that night with him that made me forget everything."

Rhonda pursed her lips. "I'll see what I can do," she said.

———

To avoid a confrontation with Calvin, Elizabeth asked Rhonda to drop her off at the end of his street. Elizabeth reached the edge of the driveway and barely noticed the man coming toward her down the sidewalk from the other direction.

"Excuse me," he said.

The voice caused Elizabeth to stop.

It was Crazy George. But he was out of his hospital uniform and looked like a successful businessman in regular street
clothes.

"We need to talk," he said in a low whisper.

"What?"

"Can you get out tonight — to take a walk?" he asked firmly.

She was taken aback, and stammered, "Look, I'm working
really hard to figure things out right now. And, no offense, but
your channel-switching-coincidence-mumbo-jumbo stuff isn't
helping me cope with my life now."

He didn't seem to hear her. "Meet me out here around eight.
We have to talk. It may be a matter of life and death."

"Yeah? Whose?"

"Yours."

23

Malcolm rubbed his eyes wearily and wondered how long he'd been watching this last group of patients through the one-way glass. He looked at his watch. Nearly 10:00 p.m. He should have called Jeff long before this to follow up on their conversation about the mysterious T-shirt. Jeff had searched the Internet with no luck, so Malcolm had suggested that he check with Jerry Anderson at the *Gazette*.

He picked up a mug imprinted with "St. Agnes Mental Facility" and sipped the coffee. It was cold.

Dr. James Weyhauser, a good friend of Malcolm's and now a psychiatrist at St. Agnes, stepped into the room quickly and closed the door behind him. His movements were jerky but precise. He reminded Malcolm of a stork. "Well?"

"Coffee's cold," Malcolm said.

"Forget about the coffee. What do you think?"

Malcolm looked again at the group of patients. They were seated in a semicircle, talking to a staff therapist about their lives and memories. "They're psychotic, insane, schizophrenic, or — "

"Or what?" Jim dropped into a chair next to Malcolm and shoved his hands into the pockets of his white lab coat.

Malcolm scrubbed his chin. "That's the question, isn't it?"

Indeed it was. Jim and Malcolm enthusiastically shared an

interest in unexplainable phenomenon; they had met in Oxford during a conference on that subject. In this case, Jim had assembled a group of people who were being treated as amnesiacs. Yet, unlike most amnesiacs with short-term or long-term memory loss, these seemed to have very detailed memories apart from their documented lives.

"I thought you'd be interested in this group because their so-called fictitious memories have commonalities," Jim said.

Malcolm tugged at his ear thoughtfully. "But the commonalities are actually *uncommon*. They're remembering places and events that have no point of reference in society as we know it. It's as if they've made up their own little worlds."

Jim raised a finger. "*And* their own identities in those worlds. Each of them keeps insisting that he or she is someone else. That's what intrigues me and what made the other doctors glad to be rid of them. They think it's the same condition that leads the mentally ill to delusions of being Jesus or Napoleon. But I say this group is different."

"Where did they come from?"

"All over the country," Jim said. "They were sent to me because I expressed an interest in cases like these at our annual conference last year."

"Is it possible they aren't deluded? Is it possible that they are who they say they are?"

Jim spread his hands. "I haven't the slightest idea. But *they* sure believe they are who they say they are."

"So what's the answer?" Malcolm asked.

"I've been waiting all night for you to say the obvious." Jim smiled.

"The obvious." Malcolm looked perplexed.

"What are you always harping about?" Jim prodded. He groaned when Malcolm didn't reply. "*Time*, Malcolm. You're always harping about time — how we don't understand it — how there may be more to it than our here-and-now perspective.

I was betting that you'd bring it up as an explanation for these people."

Malcolm honestly hadn't thought about it. "Other lives, other times," he mumbled mostly to himself. "I toy with the idea of an alternative time. I thought I had another case in Fawlt Line, but ..." His voice faded. Immediately, he regretted referring to Elizabeth as "another case."

Jim brought their discussion back on track. "They give every appearance of being normal except that they remember lives, events, and places — an entire world that's different from what we know about them. How is that possible, if they aren't psychotic or paramnesiac? Have they slipped a notch and gone too deeply into their own imaginations, like an author who suddenly *lives* his books?"

"Maybe, but that's a psychological question. You can answer that better than I can."

"Don't give up so easily," Jim said, a challenge in his voice.

Malcolm sat up, his mind shifting into a higher gear, and he began to speak quickly. "Right! Then let's say that these people really are remembering some other time, some other life they once had. Did they cross over from that time? If so, how did they do it? Did they just simply invade someone else's brain? Or is it possible that their minds snapped in the process?"

"So you think they are insane? They're from another time, but lost their minds in the crossover?"

Malcolm shrugged. "Or perhaps there's a physical transfer somehow." He stopped, realizing the insanity of their entire conversation. How could someone physically switch from one time, or alternate time, to another?

Jim said, "There's no evidence that any of these patients are someone other than who their birth certificates say they are. Their families know them. If people were physically jumping back and forth in time, we'd see the difference, wouldn't we?"

"Hm," was all Malcolm could say.

The two men sat quietly for a moment. Finally, Jim clapped his hands on his knees and stood up. "Let's try The Hypnosis."

"The Hypnosis?" Malcolm rose and followed his friend to the door.

"We've been developing a new type of hypnosis in our clinics in California," Jim explained as they walked. "I won't bore you with the details. It's an experimental approach that taps into a patient's subconscious dream-state without sending the patient to sleep. We're able to bypass the mental and emotional filters and get to the place where the subconscious, dreams, even feelings of dèjá vu are located. The *pontine tegmentum*."

"Thanks for not boring me with details," Malcolm said.

Jim smiled. "I could have given you a lot more than that. Anyway, it lets a person enter into the realm of dreams — not memory, mind you — and allows us to talk to him while he's there."

They walked down a hallway, jogged left, then right into a corridor. Malcolm felt like a rat in a maze.

"Does this form of hypnosis have a name?" Malcolm asked.

"Well, if it works, I was thinking of calling it the Weyhauser Technique."

"Catchy," Malcolm said.

24

Calvin's parents escaped to watch television while he and Elizabeth cleared the dinner dishes from the table. It had been her first meal with the entire family, and she prayed it would be the last. Except to ask her to pass the butter, they didn't speak to her. Even Calvin seemed lost in a broody silence, broken only when she asked him about his day at the bank. He told her a lot more than she wanted to know about the stock exchange.

"How was *your* day?" Calvin asked when the last of the dishes were put in the dishwasher.

Elizabeth shrugged. "It was okay. I followed doctor's orders and looked through my room."

"Find anything interesting?" he asked. But it was a fake question, Elizabeth could tell. He was leading her. Somehow he already knew the answer.

"Nothing that helped me remember anything," she answered.

Her back was to him as she rinsed out a pan, but she felt his eyes on her.

"Did you go out today?" he asked.

She dropped the pan into the bottom of the sink with a bang. "Sorry," she said. "It slipped."

Calvin's voice was taut. "Y'know, I'm not sure you should go out. I don't think Dr. Waite wants you wandering around town alone."

But I wasn't alone. You know I wasn't alone. You know I was with Rhonda. Were you following me again?

Calvin continued, "You should wait until I come home, and we'll go out together."

"But I like to be alone," Elizabeth said.

"It's not good for you," Calvin snapped.

She recognized the angry tone in his voice, and it frightened her. *How do I tell him that I want to take a walk without him tonight?*

"You worry too much," she said pleasantly and strode out of the kitchen.

He followed her as she walked toward the living room. Seeing his parents, she made a hasty turn to go up the stairs to her room.

"Where did you go today?" he demanded.

"Calvin, what's wrong with you?"

"Nothing's wrong with me. I asked a simple question."

Elizabeth turned on him. "I'll answer your question if you'll answer mine. What happened the night I lost my memory?"

The question stopped him cold. "What?"

"I'm trying to put the pieces together, and it would help a lot if you'd tell me what happened that night." She resumed her trek up the stairs and went into her room. He followed close behind.

"You're changing the subject," he said angrily.

She stopped in the center of her room. "You're right. So how about telling me. You said at the hospital that I went to the movies alone."

He leaned against the door frame and shoved his hands into his pockets. "I made that up so the doctor wouldn't start asking a lot of embarrassing questions."

"Embarrassing for whom? You or me?"

"Both of us."

"Where did I go, Calvin?"

"You said you were going to run away — and that's what you did. You left. I thought you meant it this time." He hesitated. "Until you showed up later. Boy, was I surprised. And then I was even more surprised when you didn't know who you were."

His anger had subsided now. The memory of that night seemed to have made him anxious about losing her again, just as she had known it would. She wondered if Sarah used to manipulate him the same way.

"Where did I go that night?" she asked.

Calvin chewed his lower lip. "I don't know. You didn't tell me what you were plotting to do."

"Calvin!" his mother called from downstairs.

"Yeah?" he shouted back.

"Is it too much to expect you to wipe off the table?"

He rolled his eyes and jerked away from the door frame. "No, Mom. I'll be right down." He ambled away.

Elizabeth glanced at her clock. It was twenty past eight. She went to the window and looked out into the night. If Crazy George was out there, she couldn't see him. She felt bad that she couldn't go out to meet him, but she didn't dare suggest to Calvin that she take a walk alone. He would go through the roof.

The moon and clouds cast shifting shadows on the street at the end of the driveway. The effect almost made her believe she could see someone standing down there. She sighed and turned away from the window. A matter of life and death, Crazy George had said. She tried to shrug it off. He'd only give her another lecture about TV channels anyway.

She threw herself onto her bed, and her eye was caught by a picture on the nightstand. It was of her and Calvin eating cotton candy at a carnival.

What went on the night I ran away? she wondered. *I ran away and then came back without my memory. Where did I go in the meantime? What happened to me?*

25

Sheriff Hounslow threw the morning edition of the *Gazette* onto the table and scowled. "It's ridiculous!" he said as he navigated his sturdy frame into a chair. "If that boy thinks he's going to get off as my prime suspect because of a rock and jazz festival, he has another thing coming."

Hounslow was referring to Jerry Anderson's column about the mystery of Elizabeth's T-shirt. The reporter had done a thorough check into the Montfair Rock and Jazz Festival and couldn't find it anywhere. It didn't exist.

Officer Peterson, Hounslow's right-hand man, scratched his bald head. "I've looked everywhere too. Online, offline, inline, outline. No one anywhere has ever heard of the Montfair Rock and Jazz Festival."

"So someone made it up. The T-shirt was a joke," Hounslow growled.

"Mr. and Mrs. Forde said they'd never seen the shirt before. And since Mrs. Forde always did Elizabeth's laundry, she's sure she would've — "

"I know, I know, I was *there*, remember?" The chair complained as Hounslow tilted it back onto its rear legs. "This is getting sloppy. I *hate* sloppy cases. Jeff's just trying to divert us from what really happened that night."

Peterson took a donut out of the open box on the table. "What do *you* think really happened?" He bit into the thick chocolate.

Hounslow clasped his hands behind his head and rocked gently in the creaking chair. "Easy. It was Jeff who really wanted to run away. Elizabeth agreed, but changed her mind. While her parents were at their church meeting, she went down to the Old Saw Mill in her T-shirt, sweatpants, and tennis shoes to tell Jeff that she wouldn't leave with him. Otherwise, she'd have brought clothes with her, right? Well, Jeff got angry and tried to force her to go. She refused. That made him angrier, and he lost control."

Peterson spoke through a mouth full of donut. "Jeff Dubbs is one of the most laid-back kids in town. No one who knows him will believe that he did something like that."

"It's not my job to persuade anyone of anything — except the district attorney. I just have to come up with a plausible solution to this case. Jeff was there. We found his footprints and nobody else's, so that makes him the *only* one there." He dropped the chair back down onto four legs and considered the donut box.

"But you don't have *her* footprints there either."

Hounslow scowled. "He strangled her in the mill and *carried* her down."

"It's all circumstantial," Peterson said. Then he added recklessly, "Are you sure you don't have it in for the boy? This isn't some kinda payback because Malcolm wouldn't support you in the election last year?"

"No!" Hounslow hoisted himself to his feet. "I don't think that way, and I don't want to hear anyone suggest it. I'm interested in the facts, no more and no less."

Sally, the station's phone receptionist, tapped on the door and walked in without waiting for an answer. "Kevin on line one," she said and retreated like a cuckoo in a cuckoo clock.

Kevin was the officer watching Elizabeth's room that afternoon.

Hounslow picked up the phone and punched the button. "What's up, Kevin?"

"You need to come down here right away," the youthful voice answered.

"Why?"

"The doctor was just here talking to Mr. and Mrs. Forde and the Dubbs kid. He said he went back over Elizabeth's X-rays and found something he can't explain."

"Like what?"

"Her dental work is different," he said.

"What?"

"Her dental work is different. Elizabeth had perfect, cavity-free teeth. They've got the records to prove it. But the girl in the coma has a three-year old filling in one of her molars."

Hounslow frowned. "I don't get it. Her fingerprints are identical. Her parents — everyone — who has seen the girl has given positive identification. What does her dental work have to do with anything?"

"I'm just telling you what the doc said," Kevin stated. "Everything checks out except her teeth. Her parents and her dentist say there's no way she ever had a filling." Kevin paused for a moment. "They're saying this girl may not be Elizabeth."

Hounslow slammed the phone down.

26

"Thanks, Jeff," Malcolm said and placed the phone receiver back on the cradle. The afternoon sun streamed through the half-closed blinds on the window. His head ached from too little sleep and too much thinking. He and Jim had been up late the night before testing the "Weyhauser Technique" of hypnosis on two of the patients. Apart from rambling stream-of-consciousness talking about their dreams and fantasies, the technique didn't give Malcolm or Jim any new information.

"News?" Jim asked from across his desk.

"Elizabeth — the girl I told you about — may not be Elizabeth," he said.

"What's that supposed to mean? Either she is or she isn't."

Malcolm tugged at his ear. "Not necessarily. From all appearances she is. But they found an inconsistency with her dental records that they can't explain — the sudden appearance of a filling she never had. And they still haven't been able to explain the T-shirt she was wearing when they found her."

"The rock festival," Jim nodded.

"This is a very strange situation," Malcolm said.

Jim smiled. "Well, you know weird better than anyone. Come on, it's two o'clock."

"What happens at two?"

"I want you to meet a patient we brought in this morning."

131

The patient, Malcolm learned on the way to the interview room, had been brought to a clinic in Detroit by his wife. After several weeks of examinations, the staff psychologist suggested they go to St. Agnes to meet with Dr. Weyhauser.

"He's not violent," Jim told Malcolm at the door. "Just confused. He claims to be a man named Frank O'Mara. But all his records, wife, family, and friends say he's William Putnam. Frank O'Mara says he's a mechanic, while William Putnam was an attorney. His wife Delores found him in the car in the garage, just sitting there, claiming not to recognize anyone or anything. He kept saying that everything was familiar, but not ... right."

The interview room was comfortably arranged to look like a cross between a boardroom and someone's den. Jim introduced Malcolm and Frank/William. The patient could have been Anyman from Anytown, Malcolm thought. Thinning hair, trim mustache, nondescript mouth and nose. Put him in a suit and he could be an attorney. In a smock, he might be a butcher or a baker. In overalls, a farmer or, yes, a mechanic. The only difference was his eyes. They were wide and startled, as if he were in a constant state of astonishment.

They settled into their chairs and, after some idle chitchat, Jim took the lead. "I've told Malcolm the basic facts about your case," he said.

Frank/William glanced at Malcolm nervously. "It must sound insane to you."

"Not at all," Malcolm said and picked up Frank/William's file. It contained all the details of the case, medical and dental records, and a separate folder filled with X-rays. He leafed through the papers casually. "I'm curious about where you were found."

"In the garage," the man said.

"Your wife said you were simply sitting there. Do you remember why?"

"No," Frank/William answered. "All I remember was that I was driving home from work and swerved to miss a pedestrian who'd suddenly stepped into the road. I headed straight for a telephone pole. I figured, that's it, I'm a goner. And I even figured I'd died and gone to heaven, 'cause I found myself sitting in a real nice car in a nice garage. Y'know, I'm a mechanic — I figured, what the heck, it's mechanic's heaven. Then this strange woman came out and asked me what I was doing. That's when this whole amnesia business started."

"For argument's sake," Malcolm said, "let's say that I believe you really are Frank O'Mara. Tell me what you remember about your world — the place you remember *before* you woke up in the garage."

Frank looked uneasily at Malcolm and Jim. "Dr. Carson, my therapist, said that world doesn't exist, and it's not good for me to talk about it. He said I'm an amnesiac because something awful happened and gave me a nervous breakdown. Job stress probably. I'm supposed to be a lawyer, you know."

Malcolm spoke as soothingly as he could. "Play along with me anyway, Frank. Tell me what you remember."

For the next hour and a half, Frank described his life in a town called Detroit. But the Detroit he knew was different from the Detroit he knew now. He was a mechanic who ran his own repair business. He had a wife and two sons — John and Patrick — and, as he said their names, he began to weep uncontrollably, because his memories of them were so clear. He wept as one who was grieving over the deepest loss imaginable.

Malcolm glanced at Frank/William's records and noted the conclusions of Dr. Carson. He had written that William's desire to be a mechanic might be the result of inordinate stress at his attorney's office, brought on by a major case against corrupt union officials. Dr. Carson also speculated that, since William was childless and had always wanted children, his fantasy of being the father of two boys wasn't surprising.

It's all so neat, Malcolm thought skeptically. *We have it all figured out. Everything can be explained by our doctors. An open-and-shut case.*

Having run out of things to say, Frank fell into a melancholy silence.

"What about dreams? What kinds of dreams did you have before this happened?" Malcolm asked.

"Dreams?"

"Dreams while you slept, nightmares, anything like that."

Frank thought about it for a minute. "I have a lot of nightmares now, but nothing weird before that."

"Any odd moments while you were awake? Vivid daydreams, déjà vu — "

"Day-zha what?"

"It means 'already seen,' " Malcolm explained. "It's the phrase we use to describe the feeling that we've done something before, even though we're doing it for the first time."

Frank's eyes lit up. "Yeah," he replied. "That used to happen to me a lot. It started to drive me crazy after a while." He looked down at the table thoughtfully and mumbled, "I guess it really did drive me crazy."

Jim escorted Frank/William back to his room. After a few minutes, he returned to Malcolm. "Fascinating, huh?"

"I don't know where to begin," Malcolm said. He had spread the contents of Frank/William's folder across the table. "Did you see the way he cried when he talked about his wife and children?"

"So what's your diagnosis?"

Malcolm waved a hand over the reports. "It's all here. Right under our noses. He isn't William Putnam, he is Frank O'Mara. He really is who he thinks he is."

"You're kidding."

"Why not? Rather than make him conform to who *we* think he is, why don't we accept for a minute that he is who *he* thinks he is?"

Jim slipped into a chair. "Keep talking."

"Somehow, Frank O'Mara slipped from another time and place into our time and place," Malcolm said.

Jim grinned. "And what? Took over William Putnam's body?"

"Not at all," Malcolm said and held up the file of X-rays. "He didn't take over William Putnam's body. He brought his own body with him."

Jim looked at Malcolm silently for a moment. Then he said, "But Mrs. Putnam knows him. Fingerprints, birthmarks — they're all the same."

Malcolm pointed to the medical reports. "But they're *not* all the same. The physical examination of Frank O'Mara shows that he has a scar on the back of his hand. William Putnam didn't have a scar there. Since when does someone instantly create a scar?" He grabbed the file and slid it across the table at Jim. "William Putnam had heart problems; Frank O'Mara doesn't. Putnam had his wisdom teeth removed twelve years ago. Frank O'Mara shows no sign of that surgery — his wisdom teeth lie dormant beneath his gums. How did all the doctors miss this?"

"They didn't miss it; they ignored it," Jim said. "They had to. How do you explain it otherwise? Somebody made a mistake with the records is what they probably thought."

Malcolm shook his head and thought about Elizabeth. "It's no mistake."

"Okay, bright boy," Jim jabbed. "You're saying that somehow Frank O'Mara physically slipped into our time from some other time. What is that other time: another universe? A parallel time?"

"Why not?"

Jim slung a leg over the side of the chair and folded his hands across his belly. "And you're saying that this Frank O'Mara, by an astronomical coincidence, is *what* — an identical twin to William Putnam?"

"Except for things like scars or dental work, yes."

"Then what happened to William Putnam when Frank O'Mara suddenly showed up? Where did he go? Was he obliterated by the ... the ..." He struggled for words, then said, "*alternative time twin*, or is he now in the other time being treated like a crazed Frank O'Mara?"

"I'd guess that he's probably being treated like Frank." Malcolm's head throbbed. He knew quite well how stupid this conversation sounded.

"And how did this sudden switch take place?"

"Is it possible that it happens through a dream state? Maybe déjà vu has something to do with it. You heard Frank say he experienced it a lot. Maybe that's the door through which a physical transfer took place."

Jim sat silently and gazed at Malcolm. "Do you really believe this stuff?"

"In theory, yes. It's the only thing that explains all the pieces to the puzzle."

Thoughtfully, Jim looked at the ceiling. "Yep," he said. "It sounds right to me. But they'll lock us both up if we breathe a word of it to anyone."

27

Elizabeth stood on the front porch of the Collins' house waiting for Rhonda to pull up. She held onto the rail so tightly that her fingers ached.

This afternoon she would meet David.

A car turned into the drive, but it wasn't Rhonda. It was Calvin.

What is he doing here? Elizabeth didn't want him to know her plans. She had worked hard to avoid a scene with him before he left for the bank that morning.

He got out of the car and sprinted to the porch cheerfully. "Hi, Sarah! Guess who got the afternoon off?"

She forced a smile. "How many guesses do I get?"

"My supervisor has a bunch of meetings the rest of the day, and there really wasn't anything for me to do, so they set me free. I thought I'd steal you away for the rest of the day." He smiled at her, but she couldn't see his eyes behind the sunglasses.

Her heart sank. "Oh, Calvin. I wish you'd called first. I made other plans."

"Other plans?" His smile faded.

"I'm ... well ..." she stammered, "I'm meeting Rhonda this afternoon."

"Rhonda!"

"She's helping me a lot, Calvin. Dr. Waite says — "

Calvin slammed his hand against the rail. "How can Rhonda help you? What can she tell you that I can't?"

"Nothing, but — "

"I've been patient with you — more than patient, I think!" he shouted. "I keep waiting for our relationship to get back to the way it was. Has it? No. You don't want to be with me. You're avoiding me."

Elizabeth fidgeted uncomfortably. "I'll leave if it bothers you that much. I can get a place of my own. I can afford it."

The mention of her money brought undisguised surprise to Calvin's face. He held up his hands as if surrendering. "No, wait. That's not what I meant. I just wish I could make you understand how I feel, Sarah. I . . . I don't want to lose you again."

"Then give me some room, okay? Crowding me won't make me care for you any sooner." She answered not as Elizabeth, but as Sarah. She'd say whatever she had to say to meet David. That's what Sarah would do. Yet inside, it was Elizabeth who longed to see Jeff — even if this guy was only a bizarre replica of Jeff.

It worked. The anger receded from Calvin's face, his jaw relaxed. He reached out and lightly touched her arm. "Promise me we'll have a day together soon. Maybe we could go to Watkins Park. That was one of your favorite places. Maybe it would help your memory."

Rhonda pulled up and tapped her horn. Before there was a chance to argue or discuss, Elizabeth raced down the porch steps. "See you later," she called over her shoulder. "Don't save dinner for me!"

He waved halfheartedly before entering into the house.

Elizabeth climbed into the car and exhaled long and loud.

"An unexpected encounter?" Rhonda said coolly.

"Yeah."

"You're sure you wanna go through with this?"

Elizabeth turned to Rhonda. "It's the only thing I've been sure about since I got here."

They drove into town, and Rhonda dropped Elizabeth off in front of the same café where they had met before. Rhonda wouldn't stay. She made it clear that she was not interested in seeing David again.

"Thanks for setting this up," Elizabeth said.

"I'm not sure I'm doing you any favors," said Rhonda bitterly. Then she drove away.

Elizabeth scanned the restaurant as she entered. It was crowded with young people — high school and college students — as it had been the day before and probably would be tomorrow. Her heart skipped a beat when she saw him sitting in a corner booth. *Jeff.* She wanted to run to him and cry in his arms and then wake up and know that this whole experience was nothing but a long, horrible dream. Instead, she restrained herself and walked casually to the booth, aware of how she might look to him in the cream-colored pullover and jeans. He was a stranger to her, she told herself. A stranger.

He looked up at her without smiling, and she instantly felt his aloofness. It was Jeff looking at her, but with an expression she had never seen on his face. These eyes were cold.

"Hi," she said as she slid into the seat across from him — fighting the urge to burst into tears.

He stared at her while she settled in. "What do you want, Sarah?"

His bluntness hurt her. Jeff never spoke like that. *But this isn't Jeff*, she told herself again. *It isn't Jeff.* "I guess you heard what happened to me."

"I heard. But I'm not sure whether to believe it. I figure it might be one of your stunts to cover for what you did to me. Leave it to you to come up with some stupid story about remembering another life."

A waitress arrived and took their orders for lemonade and then hustled off again.

"What did I do to you?" Elizabeth asked breathlessly, not sure she wanted to hear the answer.

"Oh, come off it," he said, and slid toward the edge of the booth as if he might leave.

Instinctively, she reached across the table for him. "Wait, please. Don't go. I need your help. You're angry with me and I don't know why. I don't know *anything*. You have to believe me. It's not a stunt."

He settled back into his seat and looked at her skeptically. "Okay, I'll play along. You were going to leave Calvin and meet me at the Old Saw Mill by the river."

"The Old Saw Mill?" she gasped.

"Oh, you remember that, huh?"

"It's the only thing I remember," she answered.

Again, he looked at her as if he didn't believe a word she said. "You were supposed to meet me there. But it was do-or-die."

"Do-or-die?"

"We agreed that if you didn't show, our relationship was over," he explained.

"Why did we say that?"

"Because I was tired of your games," he said. "You kept going back and forth between Calvin and me. You wouldn't make up your mind. So I said, this is it. Now or never. I waited for two hours, and you never came. I promised myself I wouldn't see you again. I'm only here to find out if this whole amnesia thing is some kind of trick."

The waitress brought their glasses of lemonade. Elizabeth picked hers up, but her hand was shaking so badly that she put it down again.

"It's no trick," she whispered.

David looked at her, his steely expression softening. "Then

why meet with me?" he asked. "You don't remember me. Why bother?"

She fumbled in her handbag for a moment and pulled out the photo of him she had found in the Bible. He looked at it indifferently. "Yeah? So?"

"So ..." It was too late. The tears had come and would not be stopped. "You look exactly like someone I knew in my *other* memories."

David's wall of skepticism seemed to crumble. "Now, don't do that. Don't make a scene." He instinctively left his seat, came around to her side of the table, and slid in next to her. She buried her face in his shoulder, and he put his arm around her and pulled her close.

From across the street, half hidden by a phone booth, Calvin watched.

———

Elizabeth spent the rest of the afternoon with David. She knew it wasn't really Jeff, but she wanted to stay near him all the same. He took her to Magnolia Park — an acre of trees and well-kept gardens and arteries of zigzagging paths filled with joggers, bicyclists, playing children, and lovers on blankets. In *her* Fawlt Line, the old bank sat where this park was. This Fawlt Line was more city-like than the one she knew.

David told her about his life at a private boarding school. His parents, who according to him were too rich to pay him any attention, had put him there to get rid of their guilt. He told Elizabeth how he had met her — Sarah, that is — at another friend's birthday party. The party got out of control, so David, Sarah, and Rhonda had slipped back to Rhonda's house. "What a pair you were. You kept me laughing all evening," he said with a smile. "I fell for you right then and there."

"Weren't you already going out with Rhonda?" Elizabeth asked.

David laughed as if she were joking. "What do you mean?"

"Rhonda said that I stole you away from her."

David looked puzzled. "Rhonda and I were never a couple. You must have misheard her."

Elizabeth was sure that she hadn't, but she didn't say so. Why would Rhonda lie to her? Or was David the one lying?

28

"This is nuts!" Jeff cried out. He and Malcolm were in the den at the cottage. "Time twins ... alternate worlds ... it sounds crazier than all that other junk you told me."

"It's the only explanation that makes sense. I defy anyone to explain the dental work and the mysterious rock festival on that girl's T-shirt," Malcolm said.

"*That girl* is Elizabeth," Jeff said.

"Perhaps not. Even the doctor is confused about — "

"Do me a favor, okay?" Jeff interrupted. "When they arrest me, don't bring any of this up at the trial. I mean it, Malcolm. They won't even bother with a jury. They'll certify us both and send us far, far away."

"You're not getting it," Malcolm complained.

"No, I'm not. How can I? You're telling me that the girl in the hospital *is not Elizabeth.*"

"I thought you'd be happy to hear that."

"Why would that make me happy?"

"Because that means she may be alive and well somewhere."

"*In another time!*" Jeff said, throwing his hands up. "And you still haven't said how she got there or how we can get her back."

Malcolm went on. "If they're time twins and they swapped

places, maybe it was through a dream-state or déjà vu. You know what déjà vu is, right?"

"Yeah, I know," Jeff said. "I get it all the time."

Malcolm was surprised. "Really? You never told me."

Jeff shrugged impatiently. "Why would I?"

"No reason, I suppose. Did Elizabeth?"

"Beats me," Jeff replied. "It's not something we talked about."

Malcolm looked disappointed. "Too bad."

Jeff groaned. "Malcolm, *please!*"

"All right, all right." He gestured for Jeff to calm down. "Let's pretend for a moment that Elizabeth passed through a doorway of time — whatever it is — at some point in the evening she disappeared. While she took a bath is my guess."

"Why then?" Jeff asked, still not believing any of it.

Malcolm tugged at his ear. "Because of the patients I saw at St. Agnes. They all have a common link between their last memory and how they were found. Frank O'Mara was in his car driving home, his "twin" William Putnam was sitting in a car in his garage. Maybe he had just pulled in. Anyway, the car is the link."

"What's that have to do with Elizabeth?"

"Elizabeth had a bath, the comatose girl was found by the river. They were both immersed in water. That's a common link. What else do we know?"

"I don't know anything," Jeff said.

"O'Mara was headed for a life-threatening situation when he switched with Putnam."

Jeff frowned. "Hold it. You said Putnam was sitting in his car in the garage. That doesn't sound life-threatening to me."

Undaunted, Malcolm went on. "Perhaps *both* sides don't have to be in a life-threatening situation when the switch happens. Putnam had a heart condition. Perhaps he had a heart attack when he pulled into his garage."

"That's a real stretch, Malcolm."

"I know it's a stretch, but I only have half of the story. I can't say what happened to Putnam on the other side. Who can? The people in the alternative time might notice the change in his dental work or scars or the sudden appearance of a heart condition, but they'd write it off as an unsolvable mystery because the fingerprints are identical. Poor William Putnam is probably being treated there the same way Frank O'Mara is being treated here: like a lunatic."

Jeff winced. "Which means that *if* your theory is true, Elizabeth is being treated the same way. Are you trying to make me feel better?"

"I'm trying to get at the *truth*, Jeff," Malcolm snapped.

"Okay," Jeff said, backing off.

Malcolm paced. "The girl from the alternate time must have been in a life-threatening situation and switched with Elizabeth when Elizabeth was in a relaxed mental state in the bath."

"It's crazy, Malcolm."

"Of course it is, but what if it's the truth?"

"But if it's true, why don't people keep switching back and forth all the time?"

Malcolm ran his fingers through his salt-and-pepper hair. "That's an excellent question."

Jeff felt like a student who'd just been patted on the head. "Thanks, but what's the answer?"

"I don't know," Malcolm said. "Perhaps there are only a handful of people with so-called *time twins*. And, perhaps, the specific circumstances for a switch are so exact that it rarely ever happens. How many life-threatening situations do any of us *really* encounter? Not many."

"So this isn't going to help us," Jeff said.

Malcolm sighed deeply. "I don't know how to prove any of it. Even if I could, it wouldn't help us cure whoever the girl in the coma is — or bring Elizabeth back."

The thought hung in the air between them, creating a cloud of despair. Suddenly the two of them looked at each other: a realization.

Malcolm frowned. "If the comatose girl from the other time was injured because someone tried to kill her ..."

Jeff picked up the thread, "And Elizabeth is in that alternate time alive ..."

"Then whoever hurt the comatose girl is in for a big surprise."

"More than a surprise!" Jeff's eyes grew wide. "They may try to kill her again!"

29

Calvin dropped Elizabeth off at the hospital the next afternoon for her therapy group. He'd been in a quiet mood ever since the previous day, and she couldn't help but wonder if he somehow knew about David. But how could he know?

"You have cab fare for the ride home?" he asked.

She held up a small wad of cash he had given her. "Right."

"I'll see you back at the house. You *will* be home tonight, I hope."

She nodded. She and David hadn't made any specific plans to see each other again. She knew only that she *would* see him somehow. He was a lifeline to her, even if he wasn't really Jeff.

Calvin wouldn't look at her, fixing his gaze instead on the line of cars parked ahead. She wanted to say something to lighten his mood, but she didn't have the time or the inclination to play that game. It scared her to think how good she might become at manipulating him. *Is that how Sarah coped*, she wondered, *manipulating him in and out of his moods?*

He rubbed his hands against the steering wheel as she closed the passenger door. His quietness made her suspicious. *It's as if he's made a decision ... as if he has resolved something in his mind that he won't tell me about.*

She made it as far as the main elevator in the hospital when she was joined by Crazy George. He stood next to her at the door as if he were just another would-be passenger. The bell chimed, the arrow lit up, and the doors opened. They both stepped in.

After the door closed, he turned to her. "I've been looking for you."

Elizabeth didn't face him. "I'm sorry I didn't come out the other night. I couldn't."

"Couldn't or didn't want to?" he said sharply.

She frowned. "Am I obligated to you?"

He took a step back from her and spoke in a measured tone. "Something is going to happen. Everything in my bones tells me that a change is about to take place again."

The elevator stopped, and an orderly stepped in. She smiled at them both and then faced the doors. They all waited in silence until the next floor, where Elizabeth and George stepped off.

"What kind of change?" Elizabeth asked as they walked toward her meeting room.

"The last time I felt like this was the night you had your amnesia: the night Sarah became Elizabeth — or vice versa."

Elizabeth rolled her eyes. "A feeling in your bones. Switching TV stations. Why should I believe any of this stuff?"

"You should believe me because I believe you," he said. "You're no more Sarah Bishop than I am Abraham Lincoln. Now listen to me. Something is going to happen; things are going to change. We need to stay close. Meet me tonight."

"It's impossible," Elizabeth said as firmly as she could. "I can't get out tonight, and I wouldn't want to anyway. This whole thing is nutty."

Before he could reply, she pushed on the door and entered the therapy room.

Dr. Waite and his collection of the maladjusted smiled happily at her.

I'm in pretty poor shape when this group is my only escape, she thought.

———

After an hour of verbal spewing and nonsensical stream-of-con-sciousness babble, the group broke for coffee. Elizabeth was the first one out the door. She made her way to the front of the hospital, hoping she wouldn't run into Crazy George again. She went to the curb to hail a taxi. Instead, a car horn honked at her. Rhonda was waiting in her car across the street. "Need a lift?" she called out.

Elizabeth dodged the traffic to climb in the passenger side of the little roller skate.

"How did you know I was here?"

Rhonda guided the car into the lane. "I called the house and talked to Mrs. Collins. I figured I'd drive down and wait for you."

"Thanks," Elizabeth said. "What's up?"

"I want to know how your time with David went," Rhonda said bluntly. "I didn't think you'd be able to talk at home."

Elizabeth put her sunglasses on to ward off the late afternoon sun. "You can be sure of that."

"Well?"

Elizabeth wasn't sure how much to tell her. "It was good to see him. We had a nice talk."

"Anything else?"

"Like what?"

Rhonda smiled. "Like, you know, the old flame, the old feel-ings. Did he kiss you?"

"No," Elizabeth said. "I got a little worked up and cried once, so he put his arm around me. That was all."

"But you want to see him again," Rhonda said.

"Yeah, but it's not the way you think it is," Elizabeth stated. "It's different."

Rhonda turned her doubt into a tease. "Sure, Sarah. Who said it'd be different — you or him?"

"What are you talking about?"

"He's not what he seems," she answered, her tone now very serious. "He's cruel and dangerous."

"He was very nice to me."

"You went to meet him that night, and you lost your memory. If I were you, I'd wonder why."

Elizabeth shook her head. "If anything happened to me, it didn't happen because of David. He said I never showed up that night."

"He might be lying," Rhonda countered. "Maybe he did something to hurt you that night — something that *gave* you amnesia."

Elizabeth looked ahead at the cars on the ribbon of street. It looked like a black river. She had a sudden flash of that moment in her tub when it felt as if someone was strangling her, holding her under the water. The memory was so vivid that she gasped loudly and closed her eyes tight to shut it out.

"What's wrong?" Rhonda asked. "Are you all right? Should I pull over?"

"No," Elizabeth whispered. "It's okay. Just take me home, please."

Rhonda watched her from the corner of her eye. "Sarah?"

Elizabeth settled back into the seat and stared at nothing. The bath, the murky water, the strong hands — the memory left a thick residue on her feelings. She felt vulnerable. David ... Rhonda — why would either one of them lie to her? *Why?* she wanted to ask Rhonda. *Why do you think David hurt me the night I lost my memory? Why would anyone want to hurt me?*

But aloud she said, "I have a headache."

"Look," Rhonda said, "I'm sorry. I just thought you ought to be warned about David. He's not who you think he is."

But none of you are who I think you are, Elizabeth thought. *Rhonda plants seeds of doubt about David, Calvin buries an uncontrollable jealousy, David is a mystery. Who's lying? Who's telling the truth? What did I do to deserve friends like this?*

For a moment, she felt as if Sarah herself was now taunting her. *You're in over your head. This is my world, and you don't belong here.*

It was the only truth Elizabeth understood. *I don't belong here.*

She managed a faint smile and thanked Rhonda for the warning. "I'll be careful."

30

David was waiting in the driveway for Rhonda when she got home. She pulled the car past him into the garage and got out amid the exhaust fumes. Coughing, she barely glanced at him when he walked in.

"What are you doing here?" she asked, but walked on, not waiting for his answer.

He followed her through the door that led from the garage to the kitchen. It was a spacious room in a spacious mansion. The note on the counter said that her parents were out for the evening. Rhonda went to the refrigerator and pulled out a Coke. She didn't offer one to David. "Are you happy now that you have Sarah back?" she asked. Her tone was venomous.

"I don't have her back," he replied. "I don't think *anyone* has her back — not the Sarah we knew. The amnesia's for real."

Rhonda took another drink. "It doesn't matter. Now that Calvin knows she's seen you again, she'll have more than amnesia to deal with."

"How does Calvin know I saw her?"

She slid into a kitchen chair and dropped her soda can onto the table with a thud. "He's been following her. He saw you at the diner."

"So? What'll he do?" David asked.

Rhonda seethed. "You're an idiot. Calvin knew about you and Sarah long before you thought he did."

"Where are you getting all this information about Calvin? How did he know?" David demanded.

"Because I told him," Rhonda answered. "I was sick of standing by while you two played lovebirds."

David was shocked. "Why would you tell Calvin?"

"You're really blind, aren't you? It's obvious."

David strode forward and grabbed her by the shoulders, her drink spilling onto the tiled floor. He looked straight into her eyes. "What are you up to? What kind of game are you playing?"

Her eyes were narrow lines of scorn. "Get out of here."

David persisted. "Why did you tell Sarah that we used to go out?"

"I suppose you told her we didn't. Is that how you console your poor male ego, by denying there was anything between us just because I dumped you?" She laughed derisively.

"Dumped me?" David asked. "How could you dump me when we weren't even seeing each other? What are you trying to pull?"

Rhonda turned away from him and didn't answer.

"If this is another one of your schemes, it won't work," David shouted. "You and Calvin won't stop us from being together if that's what we want to do."

Rhonda laughed again. "Did you really think Calvin was going to sit back and let Sarah meet you at the river that night — or *any* night? He'd kill her first."

31

The more Malcolm thought about it, the more he realized that Jeff was right. Elizabeth was likely in danger at the hands of whoever tried to kill her time twin. *If she isn't already dead*, he thought, then quickly dismissed the idea. He picked up the phone and dialed a number.

"Jim?" he said when his friend answered.

"Hi, Malcolm."

He skipped the usual pleasantries. "I need a favor."

"What kind of favor?"

It took some doing, and he had to agree to some specific conditions, but in the end, Malcolm persuaded Jim to explain how to employ the "Weyhauser Technique."

—

Malcolm and Jeff arrived at Elizabeth's house just as the sun threw its last orange rays over the walls and garden. At the front door, Jeff stopped.

"Are you sure this is all right?" he asked. "I mean, isn't this a crime scene?"

"The sheriff said he got all the evidence he needed."

"What evidence — the bathtub and water?"

Malcolm chuckled as he opened the unlocked door. "I explained to the Fordes that I wanted to test a theory about what

155

happened to Elizabeth that night and that I needed to see her bathroom. They said they'd leave the door open for me when they went to the hospital."

They crossed through the cool foyer. Shelves full of disheveled books, middle-eastern tapestries on the walls, and a large grandfather's clock made the place look like a set from a Sherlock Holmes movie.

"That's all you said, and they said okay?"

Malcolm looked at his nephew defensively. "They trust me."

"*I* wouldn't," Jeff said as they headed up the stairs. "What theory? How is this supposed to help Elizabeth?"

"You'll see."

"But — "

"Do you want to save Elizabeth or not?"

They walked on silently. At the top of the stairs, they turned left to go to Elizabeth's room. Jeff glanced around uneasily. He felt sneaky, as if they were invading her privacy.

The room itself startled him. Not that anything was wrong. On the contrary, it was *too* right; it was her. The decorations, the posters, the knick-knacks, the books at odd angles, the photos haphazardly scattered on the dresser and nightstand were like her fingerprints on a canvas. He breathed in. The room smelled of her. He felt a pang in his chest. He missed her in the deepest part of his soul. If he could get her back, things would be different. No more "just friends" stuff. He wanted her for keeps.

Malcolm wandered into the bathroom. His voice echoed as he called out, "In here, Jeff."

Still unsure of his cousin's intentions, Jeff walked in and looked around.

"Sit down," Malcolm said as he gestured to the covered toilet. Jeff obeyed. "I'm going to explain what I want to do."

Jeff watched him expectantly.

Malcolm smiled awkwardly. "We're going to attempt to save

Elizabeth by going to the alternative time to get her," Malcolm announced.

Jeff stared at his cousin. "I don't understand."

"If my theory is right, she's in great danger. You said so yourself."

"But we're guessing," Jeff said. "It's a wild theory."

"Maybe so. But if it's a theory that's actually a fact, then Elizabeth really is stuck in an alternative time, and she may be in a life-threatening situation."

Jeff frowned. "Then what — I mean, how — I mean — "

"There is a form of hypnosis that Dr. Weyhauser taught me. I think the 'Weyhauser Technique' sounds cumbersome, don't you?"

Jeff squirmed on the toilet lid. "Forget about the name of the technique, Malcolm. Could we go back to the part about going to an alternative time?"

"If my theory is right — and I'm convinced it is — and if this technique works as it should — and I'm not convinced it will — the part of the brain that establishes a dream-state or a state of déjà vu will be stimulated through the Weyhauser Technique. I think it's a bridge that leads to an alternative time." Malcolm pulled a pencil from his jacket pocket.

Jeff gulped. "But ... what if it doesn't work?"

"The hypnosis may fail completely. But apart from a profound sense of disappointment, that's the least of our concerns."

"What else?"

He leaned against the tub and gave Jeff his full attention. "There may not be an 'alternative twin' to switch with. In which case, I don't have a clue about how to help Elizabeth."

"And?"

"I'm not sure what will become of the alternative twin if he or she comes to our time," Malcolm said.

"Okay," Jeff said. "Anything else?"

Malcolm nodded. "This is the biggest stickler of them all. I don't know how to get back." He patted his pockets, found what he was looking for, and pulled out a packet of folded pages. He opened them up and handed them to Jeff. "This is how to do it. It'll be hard at first, but I think I can reach a level of concentration that — "

"Whoa, wait a minute," Jeff said. "You expect me to hypnotize *you*? Not a chance."

"Don't be nervous. You'll do just fine."

"No. I mean, you're not crossing over."

"Of course I am. But I need you to stay close by in case something goes wrong." He looked around the bathroom. "I think this is the best place to try it. I believe Elizabeth was in the bath when — "

"You can't go. If anyone goes, it's me."

Malcolm chuckled. "Go where? You don't believe any of this nonsense."

Jeff leaned forward. "I don't know if I believe it or not, but I'll take the chance if it'll get me to Elizabeth."

"But, Jeff — "

"Look, it's more important for you to be here if something goes wrong. You can explain it to Sheriff Hounslow better than I can."

Malcolm pressed his lips together and thought for a moment. Then he nodded. "Good point. You go," he said. "But what if I can't get you back?"

"It doesn't matter. I love her, Malcolm, and I don't want to be here if she's not with me."

Malcolm smiled at his younger cousin.

Jeff blushed. "Hurry up before I change my mind," he grumbled.

"All right." Malcolm pulled a small pencil-like flashlight from his pocket that emitted a soft blue light. He slowly passed it in front of Jeff's eyes, whose lids started to droop.

"What happened to using old pocket watches?" Jeff teased sleepily.

"Old school stuff. These are modern times." Malcolm reached into his pocket and brought out a micro-recorder. He found the record button and pushed it. "For the record. Dr. Weyhauser wants to hear what happens."

"Better not make me do anything embarrassing and put it on the Internet."

"I promise."

They looked at each other silently for a moment.

Malcolm continued shining the light from one eye to another. "Okay, Jeff. I want you to relax."

"Relax. Right."

32

Calvin's face was purple with rage. He shouted at Elizabeth, but his words were unintelligible. The name "David" was all she could pick out of the barrage.

They'd gone beyond the point of no return this time, she knew. There would be no talking him out of this mood. For the first time, she wished his parents were home. She didn't feel safe.

"I don't understand you!" he shouted, pacing around her room. "We could start all over again. We could make it work this time!"

"Make what work?" Elizabeth asked. "I don't know you. I don't even know *me*! How am I supposed to know what'll work? Why are you so mad?"

"Why did you lie to me?" he demanded. "Why did you meet him like that — sneaking around, making a spectacle of yourself — "

"What?"

"I saw you together! It was disgusting!" he shouted.

"You were spying on me?"

"I was following you for your own good!" he replied. "You're vulnerable right now. You need to be protected. You don't know what David's like. You don't remember."

"What else don't I remember, Calvin? Tell me what else hap-pened the night I ran away!" Elizabeth challenged him. "Is there something *you* don't want me to know? Maybe you don't want me to remember!"

He roared at the ceiling. "You're driving me crazy!"

Elizabeth considered rushing out the door. She calculated her odds of escape and realized that he could outrun her.

He put his face in his hands, rubbing his eyes slowly. "It was perfect. We could have started all over again," he said in a half-whisper. His voice got louder as he dropped his hands, fists at his sides. "I won't lose you again."

"Listen to me, Calvin," she said through clenched teeth. "We can't be what we were. I'm not Sarah, and I'll never be Sarah. Go ahead and have me committed if you want, but Sarah is gone. I'm Elizabeth!"

Calvin's face went ashen. "No," he said, stepping toward her. With dizzying speed he reached out and grabbed her arm. "Is that who David wants you to be? Is this his idea?"

"David doesn't have anything to do with this," she started to say, but Calvin was beyond listening. He was twisting her arm.

"Where are you going to meet him — down at the river again?" he shouted, tightening his grip.

"No," she gasped. "I'm not meeting David anywhere. Now let go of me!"

He pulled her closer. "You're not leaving me for David," he said. "I won't let you!"

She wrenched her arm free and made a move for the door. Calvin seized her by the shoulder and spun her around. She lost her balance, crashing to the floor with a breathtaking thump as he moved toward her, his fists raised.

33

At first Jeff didn't feel any different ... just sleepy. His eyes closed. Then he felt warm, as if someone had wrapped a blanket fresh from the dryer around him. He felt completely at peace.

"Jeff?" Malcolm called out. But his voice was coming from the farthest point down a long tunnel.

Is this what it's like to be hypnotized? Jeff wondered.

"Do you see anything?"

"No," Jeff answered. But he had spoken too soon. A flash of lightning penetrated the darkness, and Jeff was running. He was running harder than he'd ever run in his life. His heart raced. He was panicked.

"What's wrong, Jeff?" Malcolm's voice asked. "Why are you breathing so hard?"

"I'm running up to a house," Jeff said. "*This* house. I'm running up the driveway."

"What do you see?" Malcolm persisted.

"The front porch ... up the stairs ... I'm pushing through the front door. It's different inside ... it's not this house ... the front hall is different ... I don't care ... I have to get to her ... I have to find her ... *what was that?*"

It was a scream — and it sounded like Elizabeth.

"Tell me!" Malcolm said.

Jeff gasped from his running. "To the second floor ... my

side hurts ... Elizabeth's bedroom, the door is closed ... I throw it open ... *Hey!*"

He saw a young man he didn't recognize, standing over someone on the floor. The stranger spun around to face him.

"Wait!" Jeff cried out.

"What do you see?" Malcolm asked.

It was Elizabeth on the floor — the floor of her room! Frenzied, Jeff opened his mouth to call out.

Everything went dark.

———

Jeff woke up on Elizabeth's bed. Malcolm was standing over him, his face creased with worry.

"Are you all right?" he asked.

"I saw her!" Jeff croaked through a thick, pasty mouth. "It wasn't my imagination! It was real! *I saw her!* Hypnotize me again, Malcolm. I've got to get back to her. She's in trouble!"

Malcolm put his hand on Jeff's sweating forehead. "No," he said.

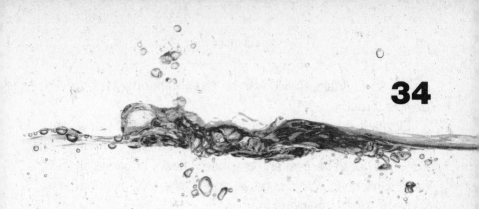

34

"Hey!" David yelled, and then leapt on Calvin. They both crashed to the floor.

Elizabeth scrambled away, trying to keep from being crushed by the two of them as they rolled around, panting and heaving, throwing wild punches that hit nothing.

She couldn't figure out what had happened. One minute, Calvin was coming at her as though he might kill her. The next minute, David was rushing through the door and leaping on Calvin like a leopard.

Bracing herself against the closet, she clumsily got to her feet and tried to catch her breath.

David was no match for Calvin, and soon he was on the bottom being pummeled by Calvin. Elizabeth screamed at them to stop. She rushed to pull Calvin off, but he swung back and hit her with the full force of his arm. It sent her into the bookshelf and knocked the wind out of her. She slumped to the ground, her breath a wheezing wind in her ears.

Then David and Calvin were both on their feet, locked in a strained, tortured embrace. Calvin pushed hard to his left, David lost his balance. Their legs tangled, and they lurched like a drunken brawl into the nightstand. The recently repaired lamp crashed down with a brilliant pop of its bulb. Then they were on the floor. Again, Calvin was on top. His hands were around David's throat.

Elizabeth screamed. It may have been Calvin and David fighting, but she saw a monster trying to kill her Jeff. Clutching her side, she got to her feet and grabbed a heavy bookend shaped like a lion's head. Without grace or skill, she swung it and clobbered Calvin on the side of the head.

He fell to the floor, moaning as he wrapped his hands around his head.

Elizabeth's legs buckled, and she fell to her knees. She saw David struggling to stand; he sidestepped Calvin to get to her. Grabbing both of her arms, he pulled her to her feet. "When he gets up, he'll be like a mad rhinoceros," he said in a raspy voice. "We have to get out of here."

Without questioning, Elizabeth let him lead her out of the house.

35

"Malcolm! You have to listen to me!"

Malcolm wasn't. He was lost in his own thoughts as he paced the room. "Think! I have to think. Did you really make it through, or did you imagine it? What did you see? What did it mean?"

Jeff sat up on the bed impatiently. "I told you what I saw. I have to — "

"Yes, yes! What you saw!" Malcolm said without hearing Jeff. "If you saw something, it may have been through your *twin's* eyes. That must be it! And if you saw Elizabeth, then it means the two of you were together. Perhaps she's in safe hands."

"No! She *isn't* safe!" Jeff cried out. "She's in trouble. I have to go back to help her!"

"I don't know . . ." Malcolm shook his head. "You're incredibly susceptible."

"I have to save Elizabeth!" Jeff pleaded. "Somebody was hurting her. *Please*. You don't know what I saw or what I felt! She's in danger!"

Malcolm stared at Jeff and made up his mind. He pulled the light pencil out of his pocket.

Jeff stretched out across the bed, and soon after Malcolm employed the Weyhauser Technique, the teen's breathing took on the regular rhythm of sleep — a deep sleep that couldn't be penetrated by Malcolm's repeated calls. All of Jeff's vital signs were normal, so Malcolm sat and watched.

A half hour slipped by before Jeff moved. At first he tossed and turned as if he were having a nightmare. Then he called out "No!" at the top of his voice.

36

David drove his car without speaking to Elizabeth. He occasionally reached up to lightly touch his bruised throat.

They turned onto Church Road. In the Fawlt Line Elizabeth knew, it was a dirt track that led to the river. In Sarah's Fawlt Line, it was a nicely paved street with modern lighted signs giving directions to the Old Saw Mill, a new development.

Within a mile, they turned right into an empty parking lot. Elizabeth could see the half-finished complex of condominiums. Even in her numb frame of mind, she was amazed at the contrast with the place she knew.

"What is all this?" she asked. "Where's the mill?"

David swung the car into a parking space close to a trailer labeled as the headquarters for the GWR Construction Company. "The *real* Old Saw Mill is over there," he said, his voice still raspy. He pointed off to the left, toward the river, where a patch of woods remained and the remnant of the old saw mill sat against a newer building. It had been restored and turned into the main office for the development. "They're putting condos in here. My father is the real estate developer in charge of the project."

"What are we doing here?" Elizabeth asked.

David held up a key. "This'll get us into the office. There's a model condo inside. I figure it's the safest place until Calvin calms down."

"But he knows about it. He knows I was supposed to meet you at the river that night."

"Unless you told him before your amnesia, Calvin can't know *where* on the river." David opened his door and got out.

"Won't someone call the police on us?" Elizabeth asked as she opened the door and slid out onto the pavement.

David joined her at the door and put his hand gently through her arm. "There's nobody here. My dad's company is suing the contractor for breach of contract. The place has been empty for nearly two weeks. You don't recognize it?"

"No," Elizabeth said. They walked to the office, and David let them in.

"This is where you were supposed to meet me the night you lost your memory. I haven't been back since." He turned on a light, and Elizabeth flinched from the sudden brightness. "I hope they haven't dismantled the room. Follow me."

He guided her past the pristine modular furniture of gray and white and the framed artist's renderings of the complex. He pushed open a wood-paneled door and turned on another light. "Ah," he exclaimed.

Elizabeth found herself standing in a picturesque model apartment that could be featured in the best home decorating magazines. *It's perfect*, she thought as she ran her finger over the cherry wood table that nicely complemented the sofa and the Chippendale chair with ottoman, all carefully arranged atop a Serapi-design rug. The colors were mixtures of rose and carnation-yellow. The room exuded warmth and comfort.

"Not bad, huh?" David said. He stood near a large fireplace on the far wall, examining his throat in the gold-crested mirror above it.

Elizabeth was horrified to see in the light how bruised and red his neck really was. "Oh, David," she said and walked over to him. "I'm sorry." Their eyes met in the reflection in the mirror. "Thank you for saving me."

He smiled. "Don't mention it."

"I'm a mess," Elizabeth said to her reflection. Her hair was tangled, and her eyes looked tired and puffy.

"I didn't know Calvin had it in him. I never thought of him as the violent type," he said.

Elizabeth was surprised by the comment. Somewhere she had gotten the impression that everyone knew about Calvin's temper.

"He has a jealous streak," she explained. "But I didn't think he'd go this far. What am I going to do? I can't go back." Wearily, she put her face in her hands. "I can't go anywhere."

David put his arm around her and pulled her close. "Poor Sarah. We'll figure something out."

"David," she whispered. "I'm not Sarah."

He smiled indulgently. "Whoever you are then, we'll figure it out." He guided her toward another door and turned on yet another light. "I think the best thing for you to do at the moment is to get some rest."

They stepped into a beautifully decorated bedroom with a four-poster bed, Queen Anne–style furniture, and another fireplace. He led her to the foot of the bed, where she sat down.

"David, I'm confused," she confessed.

"About what?"

"The night I — I mean, *Sarah* — was supposed to meet you here. You said she didn't show up."

"That's right."

"But — why *didn't* she show up?"

"I don't know. That's the question I've asked over and over."

"But where did she go? Somebody must've seen her after she left Calvin's house. I can't believe she just walked around alone all that time."

"I think it's a mystery we'll never solve, unless you get your memory back," David said. "Which won't happen as long as you keep insisting that you're Elizabeth and not Sarah. Sarah's memory can't come back if you're not her."

It was a rebuke, but Elizabeth pressed on. "Calvin said I was gone for two hours — supposedly to meet you. Then Rhonda kept dropping hints that I *did* meet you here."

"Rhonda said that?" David asked as he stepped away from her. "So who are you going to believe?"

"I don't know," Elizabeth said honestly. "None of it makes any sense. You're positive I didn't come here?"

"Positive," David said, then went into the bathroom. "I'm going to wash up. I want to put a cold cloth on my neck."

"What happened in those two hours?" she asked the empty room. She glanced around, looking at nothing in particular, until her eye caught something sitting between the dresser and the wall. It was a small black bag — a purse.

Without thinking, she slipped off the bed, stooped down, and picked up the purse. *Maybe a salesperson left it here.* Returning to the edge of the bed, she sat down with the purse cradled in her lap. She opened the clasp at the top and looked inside. It was stuffed with tissues, wrappers, receipts, a makeup bag, and a wallet. Elizabeth pulled out the wallet and opened it. Several cards fell out. Hastily grabbing them up, she saw that the top card was an identification card for Fawlt Line High School.

Sarah, heavily made up and wearing a jaded smile, looked back at Elizabeth.

Elizabeth stifled her surprise. *Sarah's purse — here?* She remembered Calvin asking her where her purse was. But, if it was here, then ... *then she did meet David here that night. He had lied to her.*

"Find something?" David asked from behind her.

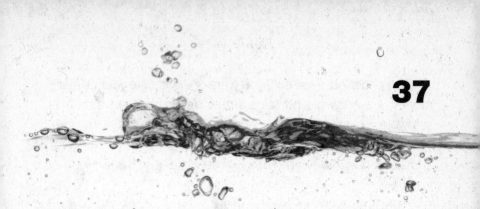

37

Startled, Elizabeth whirled around and dropped the purse. Up-ended, the contents spilled onto the floor.

David chuckled as he toweled his face. "I didn't mean to scare you."

"David," Elizabeth said, "this is Sarah's purse. I found it next to the dresser. It's been lost since the night I lost my memory."

David looked stunned for a moment and then turned crimson.

"You lied to me."

He grimaced. "Okay, it's true. You *did* come here that night."

"Why did you lie?"

David took a step toward her, his hands raised. "Because I didn't want you to remember why you came. I thought maybe things could be different if you didn't remember."

That was just what Calvin said. It was his excuse to give them a new start. "What's going on here?" Elizabeth demanded furiously. "It's as if nobody really wants me to remember that night! Why *did* I come here?"

David dropped his eyes to the floor. "You came to say that you never wanted to see me again."

Elizabeth felt as if the floor had shifted beneath her. "Wait a minute. I didn't leave Calvin to run off with you? I left Calvin to come here and say that I was leaving you too?"

David nodded. "You said you were going to take your parents' money, leave town, and start a new life somewhere else. You said you couldn't stand this place without your parents anymore. You wanted to get away."

It took a few seconds for Elizabeth to digest this new bit of information. "Then what?" she asked.

"That's all. Nothing else happened. I was angry and walked out. You stayed here. Until now, I didn't know you'd left your purse behind."

"Why should I believe you?"

"It's true," he answered.

A door slammed in the front part of the office.

"It's Calvin," Elizabeth gasped.

"Get back," David whispered. He moved quickly toward the fireplace and reached for the poker.

Rhonda walked in and surveyed the scene. She snorted. "I am so sick of the both of you. Do you have any idea the mess you make wherever you go? You're nothing but trouble."

"What are you doing here?" David asked.

She sneered at David. "You thought you could turn on the charm and I'd fall at your feet the way *she* did." She gestured toward Elizabeth. "But there was somebody better than you. He made you look like a fool."

"I don't know what you're talking about," David said.

"I hated the way you hurt him, the way you took him for granted," Rhonda now said to Elizabeth.

"The way I took *who* for granted?" Elizabeth asked.

"Calvin, you idiot," Rhonda snarled. She stepped forward, closing the gap between them. "You still don't get it. You're so selfish. But he put up with it. I don't know how he can stand you."

Elizabeth was stunned. The characters in this bizarre little play kept shifting and changing in front of her eyes. Sarah had tried to break up with both Calvin *and* David? Rhonda was in love with Calvin? What was left? "You can have him," Elizabeth said. "I don't want him."

Rhonda laughed. "A wave of your precious hand, and he's mine? I wish it was that easy."

"Rhonda — " David began.

"Calvin wouldn't listen to me," she spit back at David. "I thought he would after he saw you two at the café. I thought he'd see that Sarah was the same old Sarah, whether she had amnesia or not. She's the same liar she always was."

David moved toward her, speaking gently. "Listen, Rhonda, this whole thing has gotten out of control. We can talk about it — "

She slapped him across the face with one hand and, as he reeled back, she grabbed the poker from him with her other hand. She spun around in one deft move, swinging the broad-side of the iron rod toward David.

"Rhonda!" Elizabeth screamed.

David raised his arm to deflect the first blow from the poker, knocking it away with a painful cry. He stepped back, stumbling toward the bed. Rhonda had the advantage and quickly brought the poker back around, connecting wildly with the side of his head. David cried out as the force of the blow propelled him onto the bed.

———

Jeff's cry brought Malcolm to his side.

Enough is enough, Malcolm thought. He shook Jeff to wake him up. But Jeff suddenly slumped, his body completely limp. Malcolm bent over his cousin. Jeff had gone pale, his hair matted with sweat. He almost seemed like he was in a coma-like state. Malcolm raced to the nightstand and grabbed the phone to call an ambulance.

He had just put the receiver to his mouth when he glanced back toward the bed.

Jeff was gone.

38

Elizabeth rushed to David.

Rhonda looked shocked at what she'd done, staring at David and then the poker.

Elizabeth cradled David's bleeding head with one hand and pressed the bedcover against it with the other. "Call an ambulance!" she shouted, but Rhonda didn't move.

"Now!" Elizabeth commanded.

Rhonda seemed to relax, scowling at Elizabeth. "You were always a tramp," she said. She raised the poker again.

Elizabeth didn't wait for the blow; instead she lunged at Rhonda, catching her by surprise. As Elizabeth's shoulders collided with Rhonda's stomach, the poker came down with little force onto Elizabeth's back. Rhonda must have lost her grip, since Elizabeth heard the poker clatter onto the hearth behind her. Elizabeth drove them both onward until they crashed into the wall and then down to the floor. Rhonda, quickly rolled away and leapt to her feet. Elizabeth rolled in the opposite direction to give them some distance. She got to her feet, anticipating Rhonda's next attack. But Rhonda was frozen in place, her eyes unnaturally wide and her face white as a sheet. Putting her hand to her mouth, she staggered backward.

Elizabeth followed Rhonda's gaze. Her eyes were fixed on the bed.

David had disappeared.

———

Jeff opened his eyes and looked around. The room was dark. He sat up on the bed and had a strange tingling sensation in the pit of his stomach. Something was different. "Malcolm?" he whispered.

No answer.

He slowly swung his legs off of the bed and tried to stand. It wasn't easy. He scanned the room, bewildered by what he saw.

It was Elizabeth's room, all right, but small details caught his attention: a picture was in a different place, the bedspread had changed, a poster was missing from the closet door.

He stepped into the hall. Down on the left he saw a light coming from the spare room. *Maybe Malcolm decided to rest*, he thought, not certain of what time it was or how long he'd been asleep.

He bumped into a table that wasn't there before. The potted plant and pictures shook. He looked down and saw some photos of Elizabeth — with someone Jeff had recently seen for the first time. It was the guy he'd seen standing over Elizabeth in her room.

I'm dreaming, he said to himself.

Then he noticed the drops on the carpet. He knelt and put the tip of his finger into one. Fresh blood. His heart skipped a beat as he sprinted for the light. "Elizabeth?" he cried out.

He rounded the corner and went into the room. Suddenly, he was grabbed from behind and wrestled into a half-nelson.

Jeff struggled wildly. "Let me go!" he shouted.

His attacker spoke into Jeff's ear, his tone as casual as if the two of them were having a chat over the breakfast table. "What's wrong with you? Why did you come back?"

"I don't know what — "

The boy quickly adjusted his hold so that it was no longer

a half-nelson, but a stranglehold. It closed off Jeff's windpipe. "Why aren't you with Sarah?"

"Who?" Jeff croaked as he clawed at his attacker's arms.

"You've done enough damage. We had a second chance, but you couldn't stay away, could you?"

Jeff struggled against the vise-like grip. He kicked and clawed, until the black spots appeared and he sank down as dead weight.

At the Old Saw Mill in Fawlt Line, David woke up on an old thread-bare mattress that had been shoved into a corner. Its springs poked through the fabric, and it was covered with sawdust. His head was spinning from the blow Rhonda had given him. He gently touched a finger to a spot just above his right ear. It hurt. Through hair that was thick with blood, he could feel the gash. He wondered how long he'd been unconscious, or how Rhonda had carried him to this place, or what had happened to Sarah. He groaned as he tried to stand.

"Let me help you," someone said.

David looked through blurry eyes. A tall, slender man with a youthful face and salt-and-pepper hair reached for him. David felt too weak to resist.

The stranger put his strong arms around David and helped him to his feet. "Would it mean anything if I called you *Jeff*?" he asked politely as he guided David to the door.

David slowly shook his head. "No. I'm David."

"David," the stranger said with an undeniable sound of plea-sure in his voice.

"Where am I?" David asked as they stepped into the clear night.

"The Old Saw Mill," Malcolm Dubbs answered. "I *knew* it was part of the equation somehow."

"Equation?"

"Now let's hope that the hospital plays into it too."

"The hospital?"

"You must have your head looked at," Malcolm answered. "And I want to hear everything you can tell me about a girl in a coma."

40

Again Jeff opened his eyes and looked around. But this time he did so just as the lid of a car trunk slammed shut above him. He threw his arm upward, but it was too late. "Hey!" he shouted.

"Shut up," a muffled voice growled from the other side. He heard his abductor get into the car, close the door, and start the motor. As they drove, Jeff could hear rock music from the car radio blaring and thumping through the rear speakers. He felt around in the dark, hoping to find something that would help him break out. Under the trunk carpet he found a tire jack. He wedged the jack into the trunk lock, hoping to break it from the inside. The car bounced him around, keeping him from getting a good grip.

They drove onward. The combination of heat, fumes, and sweat was dizzying to Jeff. He felt as if he were on the inside of a clothes dryer as they bounced along a particularly bumpy road. He heard water splashing the undercarriage.

The car stopped, and Jeff heard the driver get out. He got a firm hold on the jack. *If this guy opens up the trunk, I'm gonna pay him back big time.*

There was a pounding on the trunk lid. "Anybody home?" a voice asked.

Jeff didn't answer.

"Good," said the voice. Jeff listened closely. The guy walked off.

Jeff waited and then put all his effort into breaking the lock. It wouldn't yield. His sweaty hands slipped, he tried again, and again, and finally collapsed in exhaustion.

His mind raced. What could he do except conquer the lock? He railed against it one last time with all his power, pushing, pulling, yanking, straining.

No good.

Frustrated, he cried out in a long, painful howl. "Let me out of here!"

Just then, the latch clicked and the trunk opened.

41

Rhonda's wide eyes darted around the model condominium. Sure that David was going to attack her from somewhere, she picked up the poker again to ward him off.

Elizabeth stood where she was, not sure what to think about David's sudden disappearance. Suddenly, she realized that she had a clear passage to the door. "Run, David!" she screamed and dashed away.

She raced from the bedroom, through the living room and the office, and out of the front door into the star-filled night. *Free*, she thought. *I'm free.*

"Whoa!" a voice called out. Strong hands grabbed her and yanked her entire body off the ground and backward into even stronger arms and a chest that felt like a brick wall.

"Calvin!" she gasped. "Help me."

Still holding her by the arm, Calvin let go so she could turn and face him. "It'll be all right," he said soothingly.

Everyone has gone nuts, she thought and jerked her arm away to escape. Quickly, he caught her wrist and twisted it.

"No," he said.

Rhonda, breathless and panicked, appeared in the doorway, still clutching the poker. "What are we going to do with her?" Rhonda gasped. "She'll go to the police. It's a mess! This whole thing has turned into another mess!"

Calvin looked sadly at Elizabeth. "Why didn't you stay away? Why did you have to come back if you weren't going to make it work? Why didn't you stay dead?"

"Stay *dead*?" Elizabeth said. "Did you think I was dead?"

"You *were* dead," Calvin lamented, "when I put you in the river."

Instantly, the image returned. Rough hands grabbing her, hard fingers wrapping around her throat, pressing tight, pushing her under filthy brown water.

"I figured that was better than losing you to David," he said.

All her suspicions, like pieces, snapped into place.

"No!" Elizabeth screamed, raking clawed fingers across Calvin's face as she wrenched her wrist away from him. Rhonda raised the poker, but Elizabeth spun quickly, clasping her hands together as though she was about to hit a volleyball — and slammed both fists against Rhonda's jaw. She didn't wait to see the effect, but stumbled away toward the patch of woods and the river beyond.

But nothing was as she had known it. Elizabeth cleared the woods to find herself running along a makeshift dock. She reached a wooden rail at the end of it, stopping for a moment to decide whether to jump over and risk the ten-foot fall into the water.

That moment of indecision was all Calvin needed. He caught her by the hair and pulled her back. He brought his free hand around to her throat.

"I thought we had a second chance. Your amnesia would let us start all over. But you spoiled it again," he said mournfully. Elizabeth saw the tears on his cheeks. He tightened his grip around her throat.

Pounding her fists against his chest, she tried to scream. Nothing came out but a wrenching gasp.

This is it. This is the end of what started in the bathtub. Why didn't I just die then?

She swam in and out of consciousness. Any power in her body faded as her arms flapped against Calvin like two strips of cloth in the wind.

A shrill scream sounded and then abruptly shut off.

Calvin must have heard it, because he turned away from Elizabeth to look, and his grip on her slightly diminished. With all of her remaining strength, she brought her arms up between them and punched outward to knock his hands away. It freed her from his grip, but only for a second. He backhanded her, knocking her against the rail. Instantly, he had her by the throat again. He pressed her against the railing and leaned all his weight into this final attack. She couldn't breathe. Black spots spread over her eyes like drops of oil.

There was a loud crack as the railing gave way. They both fell over the side of the dock. Elizabeth expected — even waited for — their hard splash into the cold river, but instead, they landed side-by-side with a dull thud on a construction barge below. The wind was knocked out of her, and a sharp pain shot through her wrist. Calvin groaned, then rolled over, and got swiftly to his feet. Elizabeth was completely disorientated. She tried to crawl away from him, gasping. He reached out in time to catch her blouse. The cloth tore, but now he had her arm and was dragging her toward him.

A dark figure rose up behind Calvin. "Behind you!" it called out, and Calvin turned. Like a batter swinging for a fast ball, the dark figure brought a two-by-four crashing against Calvin's skull. There was nowhere for him to go but down.

Elizabeth lay back on the barge, barely conscious. She couldn't take any of it in. Above her, she thought she could see Rhonda on the dock. David was there too, restraining her.

"Calvin!" Rhonda screamed and broke free from David, then scrambled down the flight of stairs connecting the dock to the barge. There she cradled Calvin in her arms, caressing his head.

David also descended to the barge as the dark figure moved to Elizabeth. He knelt down next to her, moving out of the shadows and into the glow from a light above. It was Crazy George.

"I told you something was gonna happen," he said proudly.

David knelt next to Crazy George, then leaned closer and pulled Elizabeth to his chest.

"David . . ." she whispered hoarsely.

"No, Bits," he replied. "It's Jeff."

42

"Boy, when you run away, you really run away," Jeff said to Elizabeth. She was lying on the four-poster bed in the Old Saw Mill's model apartment.

"Jeff?" she whispered. She had said his name again and again when he carried her up from the dock. She was certain that she was in shock — or had slipped into yet another dream world.

He leaned over and gently touched her hair. "Yeah?"

Tears formed in the corners of her eyes. "Is it really you?"

"It's me." He smiled.

Her head was swimming. "Jeff — "

"You rest until the ambulance gets here," Jeff said.

"Phone's out. I'll have to drive to a pay phone to get an ambulance and police," Crazy George announced as he entered the room. He was carrying the poker from the fireplace. "Found this outside. I guess it belongs in here." He leaned it against a dresser.

"Where's what's-his-name?" Jeff asked.

Crazy George tipped his head toward the other room. "Calvin? On the sofa in the office. I whacked him pretty good and tied him up with some rope from the dock."

Jeff glanced warily at the office. "Is he going to — "

"Behave himself?" Crazy George smiled. "He's like a whipped puppy. He'll be fine."

"He probably has a cell phone. If it's not on him, then check his car," Jeff suggested.

"Good idea. I'll let him lead the way." He paused at the door. "It's the other one I'm worried about — the girl. She took off."

"Probably far gone," Jeff said. He winced as his cuts and bruises came to life.

Crazy George frowned. "I'll call for help, then come right back. Okay? You'll be all right?"

Jeff nodded.

George's face suddenly brightened up with a smile he'd obviously been restraining for a while. He looked around to make sure Calvin wasn't eavesdropping. "So, be honest now. You're from the other time, aren't you?"

"I guess I am. I mean, *we* are."

George clapped his hands together and laughed. "Thank God, thank God. I knew I wasn't crazy."

"I guess somebody switched the channels," Elizabeth said weakly from the bed.

"I guess so," George said.

Good old George, she thought. *He wasn't crazy after all.* She looked at him a moment. It surprised her to suddenly be filled with a feeling of deep respect for him, that he could believe for so long in something he knew to be true, but that no one else believed. Her parents came to her mind — as did Malcolm. She suspected that they might be right after all with their talk about an "eternal perspective." There was so much more to life than she knew. And it took this journey to prove it to her.

George smiled as if he knew what she was thinking.

"George, how did you know about tonight?" she asked.

He stepped toward the bed. "I felt in my bones that something was going to happen. So I kept my eye on you. I followed you to the Old Saw Mill after you left the house with David. I waited for you and then got worried when that girl and then Calvin showed up." He turned his gaze to Jeff. "I heard you banging around in the trunk. Fortunately, Calvin's car has one of those jiggly flippers under the front seat, so I could let you out. 'Bout scared the wits out of me too. There you were in the trunk, when I had seen you go into the office with my own two eyes. Unless you were twins, I knew time was out of whack."

"Hey," Calvin called from the other room. "Are we going, or are you going to let me bleed to death in here?"

George rolled his eyes. "I'm coming!" he called back. Then he turned to Jeff. "I have a million questions I want to ask you. I'll be back as fast as I can." He zipped up his jacket as he spoke. It was an old leather bomber-style jacket that Jeff guessed was very expensive at one time. He glanced at the name stitched into the front, and his mouth fell open. But George was gone before he could say anything.

"Okay," Elizabeth began, trying to sit up in the bed. She winced and stayed where she was. "You have to tell me what happened. How did you get here? How did I get here? Are we in Fawlt Line? Am I still dreaming? What's going on?"

"I'll tell you if you close your eyes and try to sleep," Jeff said. "Think of it as a bedtime story."

She nodded and closed her eyes as Jeff tried to explain as much as he could about Malcolm's theory about alternate time.

Elizabeth slowly shook her head. "It's too much to believe," she said.

"I know," Jeff said.

She told him a brief version of her story — her treatment for amnesia, Crazy George, and the mystery surrounding Sarah's "last night." She knew now that on the night of the changeover, Calvin and possibly Rhonda had followed Sarah to the Old Saw Mill condo where they grabbed her after David left. Calvin, in a jealous rage, fought with Sarah, strangled her, and dropped her into the river. That's what she saw while she was in the tub. Her bath and Sarah's struggle took place at the exact same time.

Jeff shook his head. "What are the odds that all those

coincidences could happen in just the right way so that all this could happen?"

"They're the secret workings of God," she said softly, a whisper, and closed her eyes.

Jeff watched her. *I never want to take my eyes off her again*, he thought.

Suddenly, he realized that she was looking back at him. "You're staring at me," she said groggily.

He moved closer. "Can't help it," he said. He leaned over and kissed her. Then he put his hand over her eyes so she'd have to keep them closed. "Rest, Bits. We'll get out of here in no time at all."

"Will we?" she asked from beneath his hand. "Are we going home?"

He didn't answer. Now wasn't the time to tell her that there was no going home. "Just rest."

43

David refused to believe anything Malcolm had told him. He didn't go so far as to call Malcolm a liar or a nutcase, but his expression said as much. He wouldn't speak while a doctor in the emergency room stitched the gash on the side of his head. Finally, when the doctor insisted on knowing how the gash got there, he simply said he fell down.

Sheriff Hounslow and Mr. and Mrs. Forde were in Elizabeth's room at the hospital. When Malcolm appeared with the bandaged David, everyone greeted them as usual.

Hounslow was the first to notice David's bandage. "What happened to your head, Jeff?"

David stared at Sarah, still comatose in the bed, and gasped. "No," he said softly.

"What did you say?" Hounslow asked.

"I'm not Jeff," David said as he slowly moved to the side of the bed.

Hounslow looked at Malcolm. "What did he say?"

"Wait," Malcolm replied.

David knelt next to the bed. "Sarah, what did they do to you?" He looked up at Malcolm with stricken eyes. "I don't understand. I must be losing my mind. How did she get like this? Did I black out? Did Calvin do this?"

Hounslow put his hands on his hips irritably. "What's he talking about?"

"What did he call her?" Alan Forde asked Malcolm.

"Sarah," David answered.

Jane Forde looked worried. "What's wrong with you, Jeff? That's Elizabeth."

"Elizabeth!" He shook his head and moved away from the bed. "No, it can't be true. That was *her* name, the *other* Sarah."

"Are you delirious?" Hounslow asked.

David was lost in his own thoughts, stammering, "Then who's *this*? Is she really — ? No, it's impossible." His face filled with panic and he turned as if to run.

Hounslow blocked the door. "Just what's going on here?"

Malcolm laid a hand on David's arm. "Come with me, David. There may be a way to fix this."

David looked helplessly at Malcolm.

"Let's find a room," Malcolm said.

"You wanna let me in on this?" Hounslow said, still blocking the doorway.

"Yes," Malcolm said. "But you'll have to come with me."

An empty waiting room down the hall was the best Malcolm could find. He told David to sit down on the couch and dragged over a chair. He sat down opposite the wild-eyed boy.

"I'd like to hear some explanations," Hounslow said as he hovered restlessly.

"And so you will," Malcolm said. He pulled the pencil-shaped flashlight from his jacket pocket.

"If this is some kind of trick to take Jeff off the suspect list, it won't work," Hounslow said.

"What're you going to do?" David asked Malcolm, looking suspiciously at the flashlight.

"This'll help you relax."

David sat up. "I don't want to relax. I want to think clearly. I want to *wake up*."

"Wake up?" Hounslow repeated.

"This will help you wake up," Malcolm said. He looked at David earnestly. "Look, lad, you have to trust me."

"Do I have a choice?"

"No."

David nodded. "Then do it."

Malcolm turned on the small blue light.

Hounslow shuffled nervously. "What are you doing?"

"It's too complicated to explain. But you have to be quiet, or leave us alone."

"No way."

"Then be still and be quiet." Malcolm moved the light back and forth in front of David's eyes.

"You're going to hypnotize me?" David asked.

Malcolm nodded. "Suffice it to say, if it doesn't work, it's harmless," he said.

"And if it does work?"

"Then things should turn out fine."

"I don't like it," Hounslow said. "I'm getting a real doctor." He stormed off.

⌒⌒

Back in Elizabeth/Sarah's hospital room, Alan and Jane Forde quietly discussed Jeff's strange behavior. Alan was about to write it off as the result of stress when Elizabeth suddenly began to thrash violently in the bed.

"Oh no!" Jane cried out.

The girl's flailing arms threatened to pull out the IV tubes, and Alan leapt up to hold them down. "Get a nurse!" he snapped at his wife.

Jane raced out of the room and into the hall, screaming for help as she ran.

44

What's taking George so long? Jeff wondered as he dried his face with a towel. A loud bump came from the other room, and Jeff thought it was the door. He tossed the towel over the rail and opened the bathroom door.

What he saw was so unexpected that it took a second to sink in. A girl — the girl named Rhonda that he had grabbed on the dock — was on top of Elizabeth, pressing a pillow over her face. Elizabeth's pinned arms were thrashing under Rhonda's knees.

Jeff rushed forward and threw himself at the girl. His body slammed into hers, and they both rolled off of the bed and onto the floor. Jeff's head hit against a dresser, stunning him long enough to allow Rhonda to get to her feet.

"You won't win this time," she announced in a shrill voice. She looked crazed. She grabbed a marble bookend from a shelf, lifted it above her head, and threw it at Jeff's face.

He moved quickly to the right. The marble hit the floor and fractured. He felt hard chips spray the side of his face. She was on the move. He reached out, grabbing her ankle, and pulled with all his strength. She tripped, fell, and then kicked at his hand. *She's out of her mind*, he thought.

He jumped to his feet and was unnerved to see that the bed was empty. Elizabeth was gone.

"I won't be fooled again," Rhonda said. She had grabbed the

poker from next to the dresser and now held it up. They faced one another, both poised for someone to make the next move. Jeff looked at Rhonda and the poker and had a strange sense of déjà vu. He *knew* he'd done something like this before — *with her.*

She thrust the poker at Jeff, and he dodged it. She tried again, and he grabbed for it. But she was fast, swinging it back and then bringing it forward again with all her might. The weapon narrowly missed him as he dived toward the open door leading into the outer office. He skidded along the floor and scrambled to his feet. He stumbled to the far wall, lost balance, and slammed down on the couch. The wooden armrest caught him in the ribs with a loud crack. A sharp pain shot through his body, and he cried out.

Rhonda appeared in the doorway to the bedroom, the poker raised for a final blow. Just then George stepped through the outer door and grabbed her wrist, turning it sharply, forcing the poker to the floor. He brought the full force of his elbow against her face. It knocked her against the desk, scattering papers and brochures everywhere.

She cried out, cupping her broken nose with both hands and sinking to her knees.

"Thanks," George said to her. "You saved the police a lot of extra time hunting for you."

He turned his attention to Jeff, to make sure he was all right. But Jeff was gone.

45

Jane Forde raced back to the hospital room with a nurse and Sheriff Hounslow in tow. In the doorway she suddenly stopped.

Alan Forde stood next to the bed. His face was whiter than any of the sheets. His mouth moved, but his lips were unable to form any words.

The hospital bed was empty.

———

In the waiting room, Malcolm stared at the empty couch where David had been sitting only a second before. He had hoped that if, by chance, a switch took place, it would bring Jeff to that same spot. Obviously, the process wasn't so predictable.

Think, Malcolm, think. He tugged at his ear, trying to think. *Where are they? How can I find them?*

Hounslow rounded the corner into the waiting room. His face was flushed and his eyes wide and angry. "She's gone!"

"Who?" Malcolm asked.

"Elizabeth! Alan said she just disappeared right in front of his eyes!" He glared at Malcolm. *"What's going on here?"*

Malcolm thought, then smiled. "Get one of your men over to the Fordes' house. Check Elizabeth's room." Then he remembered where he had first found David. "Oh — and send someone to search the Old Saw Mill too."

Hounslow continued to glare at him.

The abandoned office at the Old Saw Mill had a desk, a chair, and a visitor's sofa. Jeff woke up — if waking up was the right phrase — slung halfway off the sofa. He tried to stand, but the pain of a cracked rib stopped him. "Ow!" he complained loudly.

"Hello?" came a voice from another part of the mill.

Clutching his side, Jeff struggled to his feet. As he opened the office door, he noticed an old yellowed calendar on the wall. "Hopwood's Saw Mill," it said. He knew exactly where he was.

Elizabeth stood in the center of the mill's work area. Jeff stepped into view. "Jeff!" she cried out and ran to him.

"Wait, no!" he warned her as she tried to hug him. "I hurt myself."

She stepped back. "Are you all right?"

"I think I cracked a rib. How did you get here? I last saw you on the bed. Rhonda was trying to smother you."

Elizabeth shrugged and then gestured to an old mattress in the far corner of the shop. "That's where I wound up thanks to Rhonda and her magic pillow. How about you?"

"Rhonda and her magic poker, I guess," he said.

Elizabeth moved to Jeff, gently putting her arms around him. "Jeff, I'm afraid to ask, but ... are we home?"

He put his arm around her. Together they walked to the door.

"Yeah, Bits," he answered. "I think you're finally home."

A police car — the blue and white lights flashing — drove toward them.

Hounslow adjusted his belt and said to Malcolm, "This doesn't make sense."

Malcolm looked across the emergency room ward. Elizabeth

was in the midst of a tear-filled reunion with her parents while a mystified doctor attempted to check her condition.

"Well?" Hounslow asked.

"Ouch," Jeff said to the nurse who was taping up his damaged rib. "That hurt."

"Sorry," she said. "That's all we can do. You can put your shirt on now."

"I want a full explanation of what happened," Hounslow persisted.

Malcolm stood silently. He cradled one of his arms, an index finger tapping against his lips.

Hounslow turned to Jeff. "How did you get from the waiting room to the Old Saw Mill?"

Jeff wasn't listening. He was watching Elizabeth. Somehow she knew it and looked back at him. She smiled and waved for him to join them. "Excuse me," he said. He walked over to her and her parents.

"Malcolm — " Hounslow began.

Malcolm sighed. "Sheriff, I can explain it to you. But I don't think you'll believe me."

"Try me."

"Okay. Let me start by explaining a theory I have about time ..."

Malcolm was right. Hounslow didn't believe him.

George hummed pleasantly to himself as he drilled the last screw into the hinge. It had needed tightening for a long time.

He heard animated talking from down the hall and looked expectantly in the direction of the sound. A wheelchair appeared from one of the rooms. In it was a girl named Sarah. She'd been in a coma for a few days and was the talk of the hospital. Apparently, she had mysteriously appeared in one of the beds in the middle of the night.

She was being released from the hospital today and, by hospital rules, she had to go out in a wheelchair. She didn't seem to mind. A young man with wavy black hair and an open, friendly face was pushing it.

"Slow down, David," she said to the young man.

"*You* want me to go slow? Since when does Sarah Bishop want anything on wheels to go slow?"

"Since now." She smiled up at him.

He leaned down and kissed her as they wheeled past George. They saw him, but showed no sign that they recognized him.

No reason they should, George thought, and put the drill down on his work cart. When he got around the corner, he found himself on the same elevator with them. They were talking happily. He hoped it would last. There were trials ahead, he had read in the morning paper, and they'd both be part of them. Attempted murder, assault … Calvin and Rhonda were in deep trouble.

I wonder how it'll all turn out.

Oblivious to him, they got off at the lobby. George continued to the basement where he made his way to a locker. He opened it and took out a lunch pail. *I'll eat in the park today*, he decided. He grabbed his old bomber jacket and put it on. For a moment, he paused to touch the name stitched on the left breast. Sometimes the name made him sad, but today he felt okay about it. It wasn't just some name. It was a name with a history, with memories. He knew it now as surely as he knew anything. And even though people called him George, he knew that the stitched name was *his* name.

Charles Richards, it said.

It's okay, he thought and punched out at the time clock for lunch in the park. Maybe, for some reason, Sarah and David would go to the park too. Maybe he'd get a chance to talk to them. Wouldn't that be a nice coincidence?

time thriller trilogy

out of time

paul mccusker

previously published as *Stranger in the Mist*

Read chapter 1 of *Out of Time*, Book 2 in the Time Thriller Trilogy.

1

"This is a beautiful flower," Elizabeth Forde said to her boyfriend, Jeff. She lifted the small white corsage and breathed deeply. "It's amazing."

They were in Jeff's old Volkswagen Bug, heading for the Fawlt Line High School end-of-the-year school dance.

You're amazing, Jeff wanted to say, but blushed instead as he looked her over for the umpteenth time. She was wearing a stunning pink gown with lots of lacy things around the neck and sleeves, with the white corsage he had bought for her pinned to the strap. She smiled at him and he wished he had a camera to catch her in that moment: her delicate nose, large brown eyes and full lips, all framed by the long brown hair that she'd taken extra care with earlier that evening. She was beautiful.

"What?" she asked self-consciously.

"Nothing," he said, blushing again and tugging at the collar of his ill-fitting formal shirt. He turned his attention to the road, which had strangely disappeared. "Whoa!" he shouted.

They had driven into a thick wall of fog. The open fields on both sides of the road were suddenly gone and the road itself was reduced to a sound beneath their tires. Jeff slowed down and, though the sun was setting somewhere beyond their visibility, he turned on the headlights. The beams seemed to hit the grainy whiteness of the fog and bounce back.

Elizabeth gasped. "Where did this come from?"

"I better pull over," Jeff said — and did, the gravel crunching under their tires as he came to a stop. He left the engine running and the headlights shining into the thick white soup. "Let's wait for a few minutes to see if it lifts."

Elizabeth hugged herself and shivered. "This is creepy. I've never seen fog like this around Fawlt Line. At least not this early in the evening."

"It's strange. But we're in safe territory." Jeff pointed just to their right. The fog seemed to spin and swirl around a sign attached to a chain-link fence only a few feet away. *Coming Soon*: *The Dubbs' Historical Village*, the sign proclaimed.

Malcolm Dubbs was the wealthiest citizens of the little town of Fawlt Line, the next-to-last member of a family that had been in the area for close to two centuries. Malcolm, a member of the English branch of the Dubbs family, came to America to be the custodian of the Dubbs' vast estate after a tragic accident took the lives of his American cousin Thomas Dubbs and his wife. That also left Malcolm to serve as the guardian of their surviving teenage son: Jeff.

"I never thought he'd get away with it," Elizabeth said, referring to the Historical Village.

Jeff looked ahead at the fog. It reminded him of a movie screen right before a film is about to start. "He's had his share of battles over it."

It was well known that Malcolm Dubbs had been determined to create this village the moment he moved to America two years before.

"You know that most of the people in town think he's insane," said Elizabeth.

Jeff smiled. "Sometimes I wonder myself."

"I heard them at the diner the other day." She put on an accent that sounded uncannily like old Ben Hearn. "Ya know what he's doin' with that there Village, right? He's shippin' in *buildings*, I'm tellin' ya. Brick by brick and stone by stone from all over the cotton-pickin' world. Have ya ever heard of such a thing? A museum with a few trinkets and artifacts I can understand, but *buildings*?' "

Jeff began to laugh.

Elizabeth continued her imitation of Old Ben. "Do ya know what they been workin' on over the past few weeks? Some kind of a *ruin* from England. A *ruin*! A monastery or castle or cathedral or somethin'. Why wouldn't he buy somethin' *new*? We got plenty of old stuff around here already."

Elizabeth was laughing with Jeff now.

"It must have cost him a lot of money to ship in this fog too," Jeff added.

They continued to laugh until they heard a high, shrill sound from somewhere outside.

"What was that?" Elizabeth asked, quickly becoming serious and looking around.

"I don't know." Jeff peered into the fog. "Some kind of animal."

The sound came again. This time it was closer and recognizable: the high, agitated whinny of a horse.

"Who'd be horseback riding at this time?" Jeff asked. "And in this fog?"

"I think we should go," Elizabeth said, her voice rising. She was holding tightly onto the dashboard, her knuckles white.

"Bits," Jeff said. "It's only a — "

"I've got this feeling," Elizabeth whispered. Her eyes were wide, panicked. "It reminds me of that feeling I had before."

"Before?"

"Please, Jeff — just go."

"Okay." Jeff put the car in gear and carefully guided the car back onto the tarmac. He hoped that the fog might lift or, of greater importance, that the horse wasn't on the road ahead.

"Does Malcolm have horses for the Village?" Elizabeth asked, making conversation as if to calm herself.

"Yes, but the stables are on the other side of our land."

"Maybe one got out."

"Maybe." Jeff began fumbling in his jacket pocket. "Take my cell phone and call him."

Elizabeth reached over to take the phone. Jeff glanced at her, then back to the road just in time to see a large shadow take form in front of them. As they bore down on it, a horse — *the* horse — frightened by the sudden appearance of the car, reared wildly up on its hind legs, screaming at them.

"Hold on!" Jeff shouted, jerking the steering wheel to the right as he hit the brakes with full force. The Volkswagen skidded to a stop only a few feet from the horse, who came down on all fours and then jumped onto its hind legs again. This time Elizabeth and Jeff heard a shout, and a figure on the horse's back fell onto the ground.

Jeff and Elizabeth looked at each other, shaking.

"Did you hit them?" Elizabeth asked.

"No." Jeff pushed his door open. "Stay here," he said before the door slammed itself shut. He opened it again and reached in to turn on the emergency flashers. "Find the cell phone. I think it fell on the floor when we stopped," he added.

"Be careful!" she shouted after him.

Jeff made his way cautiously towards the horse, who snorted at him and then dashed away into the fog. "Hello? Are you all right?" Jeff called out.

The fog seemed to part like a curtain, as if to present the figure lying on the road as an actor on a stage.

"Oh no," Jeff said, rushing forward. He crouched down next to the figure, a very large man. Whoever it was seemed to be wrapped in a dark blanket. The man was perfectly still and his face was hidden in the shadows.

"Hey," Jeff said, hoping the man would stir. He didn't. Jeff looked him over for any sign of blood. Nothing was obvious around his head. But what could he expect to see in that fog? He turned towards his car and shouted, "Elizabeth! Call nine-one-one on the cell phone. And bring me the flashlight from the glove compartment!"

He peered closely at the shadowed form of the man as he heard Elizabeth open her door. She was already talking into the phone, frantically giving instructions to an emergency operator. The shaft of light from the flashlight bounced around eerily in the ever-moving fog.

"Jeff?"

"Here," Jeff said.

Elizabeth joined him. "Ambulance is on its way. But they're on the line and want to know his condition."

He took the flashlight from her and got his first full look at the stranger. He had long, dark salt-and-peppery hair, a beard and moustache, and a rugged, lined face. Jeff couldn't guess an age for the man. Anywhere from forty to sixty, he figured. The man wore a peaceful expression and could've been sleeping. Finally, Jeff responded, "I can't tell. There's no blood."

Elizabeth reported Jeff's findings to the emergency operator, then asked Jeff, "He's not dead, is he?"

"I don't think so." Jeff reached down, separating the blanket to check the man's vital signs. The feel of the cloth told him it wasn't a blanket at all. And as he pushed the fabric aside, he realized that it was a cape made of a thick, course material, clasped at the neck by a dragon brooch. "What in the world — ?"

Elizabeth gasped.

They expected to see a shirt or a sweater or a coat of some

sort. Instead he wore a long vest with the symbol of a dragon stitched onto the front, a gold belt, brown leggings, and soft leather footwear that looked more like slippers than shoes. The whole outfit reminded Jeff of the kind of costume he'd seen in a Robin Hood movie. At his side was a sword in a sheath.

"Is it Halloween?" Elizabeth asked.

Carter House Girls Series
from Melody Carlson

Mix six teenage girls and one '60s fashion icon (retired, of course) in an old Victorian-era boarding home. Add boys and dating, a little high school angst, and throw in a Kate Spade bag or two ... and you've got the Carter House Girls, Melody Carlson's new chick lit series for young adults!

Mixed Bags
Book One

Softcover • ISBN: 978-0-310-71488-0

Stealing Bradford
Book Two

Softcover • ISBN: 978-0-310-71489-7

Homecoming Queen
Book Three

Softcover • ISBN: 978-0-310-71490-3

Viva Vermont!
Book Four

Softcover • ISBN: 978-0-310-71491-0

Books 5–8 coming soon!

Pick up a copy today at your favorite bookstore!

Visit www.zondervan.com/teen

ZONDERVAN®
.com

A Sweet Seasons Novel from Debbie Viguié!

They're fun! They're quirky! They're Sweet Seasons—unlike any other books you've ever read. You could call them alternative, God-honoring chick lit. Join Candy Thompson on a sweet, light-hearted, and honest romp through the friendships, romances, family, school, faith, and values that make a girl's life as full as it can be.

The Summer of Cotton Candy
Book One
Softcover • ISBN: 978-0-310-71558-0

The Fall of Candy Corn
Book Two
Softcover • ISBN: 978-0-310-71559-7

The Winter of Candy Canes
Book Three
Softcover • ISBN: 978-0-310-71752-2

Book 4 coming soon!

Pick up a copy today at your favorite bookstore!

Visit www.zondervan.com/teen

Forbidden Doors

A Four-Volume Series from Bestselling Author Bill Myers!

Some doors are better left unopened.

Join teenager Rebecca "Becka" Williams, her brother Scott, and her friend Ryan Riordan as they head for mind-bending clashes between the forces of darkness and the kingdom of God.

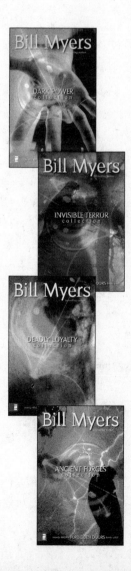

Dark Power Collection
Volume One

Softcover • ISBN: 978-0-310-71534-4

Contains books 1–3: *The Society, The Deceived,* and *The Spell*

Invisible Terror Collection
Volume Two

Softcover • ISBN: 978-0-310-71535-1

Contains books 4–6: *The Haunting, The Guardian,* and *The Encounter*

Deadly Loyalty Collection
Volume Three

Softcover • ISBN: 978-0-310-71536-8

Contains books 7–9: *The Curse, The Undead,* and *The Scream*

Ancient Forces Collection
Volume Four

Softcover • ISBN: 978-0-310-71537-5

Contains books 10–12: *The Ancients, The Wiccan,* and *The Cards*

The Shadowside Trilogy by Robert Elmer!

Those who live in lush comfort on the bright side of the small planet Corista have plundered the water resources of Shadowside for centuries, ignoring the existence of Shadowside's inhabitants, who are nothing more than animals. Or so the Brightsiders have been taught. It will take a special young woman to expose the truth—and to help avert the war that is sure to follow—in the exciting Shadowside Trilogy, the latest sci-fi adventure from Robert Elmer.

Trion Rising
Book One

Softcover • ISBN: 978-0-310-71421-7

When the mysterious Jesmet, whom the authorities brand as a Magician of the Old Order, begins to connect with Oriannon, he is banished forever to the shadow side of their planet Corista.

The Owling
Book Two

Softcover • ISBN: 978-0-310-71422-4

Life is turned upside down on Corista for 15-year-old Oriannon and her friends. The planet's axis has shifted, bringing chaos to Brightside and Shadowside. And Jesmet, the music mentor who was executed for saving their lives, is alive and promises them a special power called the Numa—if they'll just wait.

Book 3 coming soon!

Pick up a copy today at your favorite bookstore!

Visit www.zondervan.com/teen

Share Your Thoughts

With the Author: Your comments will be forwarded to the author when you send them to *zauthor@zondervan.com*.

With Zondervan: Submit your review of this book by writing to *zreview@zondervan.com*.

Free Online Resources at
www.zondervan.com/hello

 Zondervan AuthorTracker: Be notified whenever your favorite authors publish new books, go on tour, or post an update about what's happening in their lives.

 Daily Bible Verses and Devotions: Enrich your life with daily Bible verses or devotions that help you start every morning focused on God.

 Free Email Publications: Sign up for newsletters on fiction, Christian living, church ministry, parenting, and more.

 Zondervan Bible Search: Find and compare Bible passages in a variety of translations at www.zondervanbiblesearch.com.

 Other Benefits: Register yourself to receive online benefits like coupons and special offers, or to participate in research.

ZONDERVAN®
.com